DELETE, BLOCK, NEXT...

Confessions of a Serial Dater

Scarlett Sixsmith

Dedicated to all the amazing people in my life, old friends and new, who have supported and encouraged me along the way and continue to do so. There are too many to mention individually but you know who you are and I love you all dearly.

A special mention to Rachael who came up with the catchy title which, by the way, is excellent dating advice. Thank you Ms B

S x

CONTENTS

CHAPTER 1

Welcome to my story about the disaster that is my love life.

Things you learn whilst you're dating:

*The frog to prince ratio is disproportionately high.

*Chivalry is mostly dead.

*The word "gentleman" is overused.

*Short men lie about their height.

*Nobody looks like their online profile picture.

*You need a very thick skin.

*Good manners are in serious decline.

*Some men think it's acceptable to expect you to pay for your share of dinner and drinks with sexual favours.

*Penises are not very photogenic.

CHAPTER 2

"Affluent widowed gentleman 42, seeks lady of good virtue. Must have own teeth and generous bosom"

George Wilson - London Evening Gazette 1892

I like sex. Specifically, I bloody love nothing more than a bit of kinky play before being shagged senseless by a skilled cocksman. Don't get me wrong, I'm not some insatiable nymphomaniac who does things like lure workmen into my home under false pretences with the intention of seducing them with my kinky knickers before using their bodies for my own sexual gratification. Nor am I some hedonistic, knickerless, free spirit who's life is centred around fucking or a slapper with no morals. I just enjoy good sex and my level of kink is probably a little above the national average. I'm not going to apologise for that nor do I feel the need to explain myself any further.

What I am looking for is a man who can accommodate my kinky nature. Someone who is blessed with a reasonably sized cock and who knows how to use it. Although nice, I don't necessarily want presents, meals in fancy restaurants, holidays, a big wedding. He doesn't even have to love me. I just want to meet someone I like well enough. Preferably with a pleasant face, good personal hygiene and no halitosis. Someone with whom I have a little in common and get along with to enjoy a bit of company and mutual pleasure between the sheets a couple of times a week. That's all. How hard can that be to find?

It is a well known fact that when your life goes to shit it usually does so in true spectacular style. My particular story begins with the breakdown of my long term relationship something that happens to thousands of people every day. Already devastated at the loss of my dad just a few days earlier, I then found out my partner of almost ten years, Danny, had been cheating on me with some common, chain-smoking, wrinkly old tart he worked with. So much for his nicotine allergy.

A few days after dad's funeral, beside myself with grief we had had one of our usual stupid arguments over absolutely nothing at all and he had thrown the fact that he was fucking someone else in the mix. And if that wasn't bad enough he told me he had taken the opportunity to enjoy a sneaky shag whilst I had been at the hospital the night my dad died. I was utterly devastated. What kind of low life does something like that? I threw some things at him, chucked some stuff in a suitcase, grabbed my cat, and left.

To be honest I hadn't been happy in the relation-ship anyway, was totally bored and frustrated. We had no sex life to speak of, I could barely look at him most of the time without having to fight the urge to smack him in the face with something let alone shag him. But I had become a lazy creature of habit who hated the thought of being pushed out of my comfort zone and found the idea of change terrifying. Finding out he was shagging someone else gave me the bru-tal kick up the arse I needed to finally call it a day, rudely shoving me from my previous path of mundane existence and sending me careering off in a totally new but frankly terrifying direction. I quickly adapted however and it didn't take me long to come to the realisation that finding out he was shagging someone else was actually the best thing that could have happened. I was finally free of the shackles of an unhappy relationship, free to please myself and to start to enjoy my life how I wanted to.

The last time I had been single, which seemed like a lifetime ago, the world of dating was very different. It was the very early days of the World Wide Web, no broadband then, just the expen-sive bleeps, squeals and purrs of dial-up. We hadn't heard of Facebook, Instagram and the like. We only had the likes of MSN and Yahoo chat rooms in which to connect with people online. Just basic messaging, no pictures. Some people had mobile phones but they were very basic ones and there were no such thing as smartphones. I think we'd only just discovered the revolution that was text messaging. Excellent invention in my opinion, a quick text message doing away with the necessity to talk to people you really couldn't be bothered with.

There were a few early dating sites, I remember signing up to one called Midnight something or other which was just chat based no pictures. You had to rely on verbal descriptions which you would discover were mostly quite fanciful if and when you met someone in real life. If you got chatting to someone online and were brave enough to agree to meet for a date with them in the real world it was a blind date and, lets be honest here, quite terrifying.

Prior to technology assisted dating we had the Lonely Hearts ads which had been in business for many, many years. Very popular in the Victorian era when gentlemen would place ads along the lines of:-

Widowed professional, affluent gentleman seeks a lady of good virtue and genteel birth to provide domestic comforts. Preferably of full, soft but firm bosom

Since time began men have always appreciated a good roundy set of knockers.

Most of the local newspapers ran a Lonely Hearts section in their classified ads. I would imagine exploiting the lonely and the horny, especially the latter, was quite a lucrative endeavour for the publishers. It was free for women to place an ad, probably because they were massively outnumbered by the men. Also the men were more likely to respond to ads and do the chasing. We're talking the 90's, Girl Power! had finally arrived courtesy of the Spice Girls but most women were still a little bit backwards at being forwards. Publishers were obviously aware of this so they did what they could to encourage more women to participate and keep the thirsty, lonely, horny men checking the columns and ringing the premium rate numbers.

To reply to your ad the interested party would leave you a voicemail message in an inbox that they accessed by using a code that was published alongside your ad. Going off the number of messages I received when I placed an ad, single ladies under retirement age must be quite rare therefore very much in demand. It was fortunate then, that in addition to it being free to place an ad, it was also free for ladies to retrieve their messages. The ad space was limited to a small number of characters and lonely heart speak very much resembled early abbreviated text speak or some sort of war time coded message. A typical ad would be something along the lines of;

SF 32 WLTM SM 30-40 S GSOH F&F - box 6537

Which translates to:

Single female age 32 would like meet single male age 30 - 40 solvent with good sense of humour for fun and friendship

This was all potential suitors had to go on. No pictures. If they liked the sound of you from your short and usually quite generic ad then they could leave you a message. Basically if you were the right sex and the right age range they would leave you a message. As the call was charged at a premium rate the messages were invariably very short so the whole process was very hit and miss. Decidedly more miss.

One day myself and my friend Alice decided to place ads. Whether this was just out of simple boredom or frustration at the lack of decent men in our lives I can't quite remember but we received several messages some of which were quite hilarious. From offering to pay for your services (how rude!) to practically proposing marriage. Always game for a laugh we did both arrange a couple of blind dates. The most memorable of mine was with who I will affectionately refer to as the IT knob as his real name escapes me after all this time.

CHAPTER 3

From the messages I received, and there were quite a few, IT guy sounded the most promising. I called him back and we had a brief chat. He seemed normal enough, could string a sentance together, was polite enough and so I agreed to go on a date with him.

We had arranged to meet at a local pub. It was a lovely autumn day, clear and crisp and colourful, one of those days where you feel happy to be alive and are awed by the beauty of nature. I was feeling happy and optimistic when I drove into the pub car park but my heart sank when I clapped eyes on him for the first time.

It would be unfair perhaps to describe the guy as plain ugly but he looked like he'd stolen his outfit from a charity shop around 1974 whilst under the influence of alcohol and hallucinogenic drugs. I wondered briefly if he had dressed for a bet. He was wearing a bright orange and brown Hawaiian style shirt. Yes, halfway open to show off a hairy chest of course, disappointingly no medallion but he was wearing a nice ostentatious thick gold necklace just slightly more modest than a mayoral chain of office and a couple of chunky signet rings.

Paired with this delightful shirt and over the top bling we had pinstripe grey trousers so tight I could see he hadn't been circumcised, and shiny brown lace up brogues. His hair was collar length, a nondescript brown laced with chunky blonde highlights, flicked and elaborately styled, completely stiff - no doubt held with copious amounts of gel and hairspray. I think he was going for the George Michael, Wham era hairstyle which was about a decade out of fashion. He looked absurd but he thought he was the dogs danglies. He was full of arrogance, had on far too much aftershave and I suspected he was actually wearing a small amount of makeup. Almost definitely eyeliner and mascara.

I wanted to make a sharp exit just on the merits of what he was wearing but I parked up instead and, fixing a smile to my face (which I hoped didn't look too fake) walked over to him. We said our polite hello, how are you, pleased to meet yous then went into the dark and dreary pub that smelt of stale beer and cigarettes. The lovely establishment boasted a very sticky carpet, stained and ripped seating and a miserable, extremely fat barman who was leaning on the bar watching tv with his mouth hanging open. I watched the bar man go prospecting in both his nostrils, examine his finger then roll and flick his findings. I was so glad I wasn't eating there.

Things just got better and better. My date was downright rude, absolutely full of himself and a serious skinflint. We found somewhere to sit then he went to the bar where he bought himself half a coke. No offer of a drink for me.

Let me just clarify something here, I don't go on dates expecting the man to pay for everything I'm not that kind of woman, I always insist on paying my own way and I don't like to feel obligated. However, if your date goes to the bar, is it unreasonable to expect to be offered a drink? I consider myself a modern girl but I like good old fashioned manners just the same.

Sitting down opposite me, he spread his legs, well as much as he could within the confines of his ugly snug pants, rearranged his family jewels, patted his hair, cleared his throat and began his verbal onslaught. Seemingly unable to make eye contact or remember my name he called me "babe" or "doll" and talked incessantly to my tits about himself and just how wonderful he was. It's a fallacy that women talk more than men, I can tell you. The number of men I've met on dates who wax lyrical on their favourite subject - themselves, barely stopping to draw breath is unbelievable. A conversation is supposed to be a two way thing but I was superfluous to this particular one.

At 35 years old he was still living with his long

suffering mother something he wasn't the least bit ashamed of. In fact he was quite proud of it. Now I know and appreciate sometimes there are genuine reasons for adults to be living with their parents and I have since come across men of even more advanced ages who are back at the parental home, usually due to financial difficulties after relationship breakdowns, but his attitude was why pay for somewhere when he could live for free and have someone cook, clean and do his washing for him, "right babe"? He wasn't very happy because his mother had started to drop strong hints about him moving out. Not strong enough in my opinion. In her position with an ungrateful son like that still living at home way past the time he should have flown the nest I'd have been packing his stuff for him, changing the locks, moving house or even emigrating whilst he was at work. Leaving no forwarding address.

I could feel my eyes beginning to glaze over and I had to stifle a yawn or two as he droned on about his job. He considered his career to be very demanding and that he was very important and indispensable. On the whole his job appeared to consist of asking people if they tried restarting it, "just press ALT CTRL DEL" and laughing with his colleagues when someone had just lost a whole days work after their computer crashed. Yes he was one of those IT knobs who was paid far too much to lord it over the rest of us because having a GSCE in computer studies and a computer at home made them an expert in the scary, early days of personal computers. As they cost the equivalent of six month's wages, the only ones who could afford their own computers at the time were these social misfits. The geeks who still lived with their parents whilst the rest of us had bravely ventured into the real world and therefore were perpetually skint before we reached our 30's barely able to afford food and mortgage payments let alone expensive and then unnecessary electronic equipment.

To my enormous relief after just thirty tedious minutes or so of explaining to my boobs how amazing he was he looked at his large, gold watch and suddenly announced "So sorry babe, but I have to get going. It's quiz night at the local, can't miss that, I'm the team captain."

I offered a small prayer of gratitude, I had been trying to figure out for the last fifteen minutes how to get away. I hoped with everything crossed this hasty exit was a sign that he didn't want to see me again, but sadly not. "So doll" he asked "you wanna see me again?"

"It was really nice to meet you" I politely lied "but sorry, no, I don't think you're for me, there's just no chemistry there, not for me."

One thing you learn is, it is really important when you are dating to be honest and just say "No thanks" and not "Yes that would be nice" when you don't want to see them again. Even if they're really into you and you feel mean you just have to be honest and say they're not for you otherwise you will just get mithered to death. Trust me, it is easier and less painful to get rid of infected ingrowing toenails than it is to get shut of some of these undesirables if you give them even the tiniest sliver of hope to cling to. You have to be cruel to be kind and not give them false hope.

So back to the lovely charmer who was announcing to the twins "Well that's a shame, I thought we got on great."

How he had come to this conclusion I have no idea as I had barely managed to squeeze in two words during his tedious, self applauding monologue. He went on to say "I had something I wanted to show you in the car. Would you like to see it anyway?"

Yes, yes, I know I should have known better but curiosity got the better of me, and I know it would have gotten the better of you too so don't pretend otherwise. I said "Hmm, OK then" and over we strolled, with some trepidation on my part, to his car.

Of course his car was a tiny, flashy, impractical, convertible, two seater, sporty penis extension. In fire engine red. I didn't get in, I wasn't that daft or that agile for that matter. Having been blessed with the grace of a baby elephant and a having a dodgy hip even back then I couldn't see an attempt at me getting into something so tiny and low to the ground ending up anything other than painfully embarrassing.

He reached inside the penis extension, unlocked the teeny tiny glove-box and pulled out a teeny tiny video camera. Remember this was pre-smartphones. Switching it on he winked at me then proudly showing me the tiny screen the creepy little bugger showed me a film of himself having a wank in close up and full techni-colour.

Well, seriously. I mean what do you even say to that? "Thank you very much, I'm delighted that you shared that with me. You have a very nice penis. I need to congratulate you on your masturbation technique, nice wrist action?"

Anyway, it was very romantic, the perfect end to a perfect first date. Not. Flustered and a little traumatised, I said goodbye and hurried back to my car making a fast getaway swearing to myself that I was never, ever going on a blind date ever again.

Later that evening Alice came over and we debriefed over a couple of glasses of wine. She doubled over with laughter when I told her what had happened almost spraying a mouthful of Chardonnay all over my new carpet when I got to the part with the camcorder. She thought it was hilarious and laughed so much I thought she was going to have a fit. She'd got flowers on her date, who was the perfect gentleman and rather sweet she said but about 10 years older and 6 inches shorter than he'd claimed to be. He also had a bad twitch in his right eye which made him look like he was constantly winking at everyone and a very obvious hair piece. I didn't get flowers, didn't even get a drink but I did get a moving dick pic long before dick pics were even officially invented. Such a lucky girl.

Fast forward a month or so and I received a phone call. IT knob "Hey babe, I've got my own pad now, how do you fancy bringing those amazing tits over and helping me to warm up my new bed?"

Erm, now then let me think about that for a moment. Nice offer thanks but I think I'll pass. I had given him absolutely no hint whatsoever that I was into him, hadn't spoken to him since that memorable first date but here he was seriously thinking I might consider going over and having sexual contact with him?! Honestly, what kind of disillusioned idiot was he? Was he going down a list of all the women he'd met hoping he'd find one desperate enough for him to get lucky?

But hey, congrats to the long suffering mum for finally getting him to move out. I do sometimes wonder what happened to him, I bet he was ecstatic with the invention of camera phones, instant share dick pics and wank videos a plenty!

CHAPTER 4

"I met my love by the gasworks wall
Dreamed a dream by the old canal
I kissed my girl by the factory wall"

DIRTY OLD TOWN - THE DUBLINERS

After a couple more lonely heart blind dates that were non-eventful and frankly both boring and tedious my life as a singleton finally came to an end when I met Danny the good old-fashioned way, pissed up in the pub.

It was St Patrick's Day and we were both roaring drunk on green beer and Irish whiskey. Along with everyone else in the crowded, noisy pub we were celebrating our links to the Emerald Isle no matter how tenuous, lubricated with abundant amounts of Jamesons and Guinness whilst singing along boisterously to some very loud, Irish music. Feet were tapping, pints were being sloshed around all over the place, everyone was having a grand old time. Even men who'd never even crossed the Irish sea were stood with their arms around each other, swaying and spilling their pints, tearfully and tunelessly reminiscing about the girl they'd left behind in Galway or some such shite, singing along with the four piece band who were really rather good. The band members were ruggedly handsome the lead singer looking like he could have fronted a boy band. Green crepe-paper streamers hung from the ceilings, scary looking cardboard leprechauns grinned at us and giant shiny foil shamrocks decorated the walls. The party atmosphere was brilliant, like New Year's Eve all over again but better.

I literally fell into Danny's arms after fighting my way to the bar, him nearly falling over too because neither of us were barely able to stand up straight in our inebriated state. Apologising for nearly knocking him down and for standing on his foot, twice, (in my defence he did have very big feet) I craned my neck to look up at his face and found myself looking into a pair of lovely mischievous blue eyes. Definitely devilish. Tipping his oversized green and black felt Guinness top hat at me he grinned and said "Easy there shorty, I'd like my toes to be unbroken in the morning if you don't mind."

He had a very lovely smile. My lady loins, previously comatose, did a sleepy stretch out of interest and so I decided to make conversation opening with the obvious and very intelligent comment, "Wow! You're tall!"

He laughed "Really? I hadn't noticed" and then started to berate me as a cruel, heartless fashion victim for wearing a fake fur jacket. I laughed back and pointed out it was polyester. "Exactly" he said "Just think of all those poor innocent pollys that had to die to make your coat!"

We got chatting, well more like yelling at each other over the racket. It turned out that Danny and I both had genuine Irish ancestors. Mine a little distant, my great grandad Tommy's family on mum's side, Danny had a little more claim to his Irishness than me with a bonafide Paddy father. He embraced the Irish culture, especially the drinking part, with great enthusiasm and had a skill which spoke of years of practice.

He told me his dad, Eamon, was a disgraced, randy ex-priest who, unable to master the vow of celibacy, was stripped of his cassock and collar when he had gotten a married woman in the family way. It was quite the scandal back in the day, even making the national Sunday papers, at least the more downmarket gossip rags. For some reason they had kept copies and Danny showed them to me one day.

Shameless Perverted Catholic Priest Seduced My Beautiful Innocent Wife!!! screamed the headlines alongside photographs of his much younger parents and the very angry looking jilted first husband.

His mum really was beautiful. Even in her late sixties she was still a beautiful lady and she certainly had been quite the looker in her day. A real sultry, dark haired temptress with an amazing beehive hairdo. She had been a brilliant singer by all accounts, married to a handsome looking successful businessman. What she saw in the shy, plain, dowdy looking man of the cloth with no worldly goods to speak of I'll never know. Love definitely works in mysterious ways - that's certainly been proven time and time again.

Father Eamon morally redeemed himself somewhat (at least in my eyes) by eloping with and marrying his then heavily pregnant lover once her divorce came through. Obviously though he was unforgiven and ostracized by both the Catholic Church and his family. The couple were told their baby was the Devil's own seed and that they would burn in hell for all eternity to pay for their sins. Nice people those religious types. The condemned couple fled Ireland arriving in England with little more than the clothes on their backs settling down to live a nice, quiet, blameless life in suburbia raising their family in peace whilst awaiting their eternal damnation. They had loved each other greatly and after all these years still did so I think they considered roasting in the fire and brimstone pits of hell a small price to pay to be together. I think those Catholics may have had a point though with the Devil's seed thing after getting to know Danny.

Danny was great fun to talk to that night and we continued to chat each other up in the usual way - trashing what the other was wearing and generally taking the piss out of each other. He made me laugh, although as drunk as I was by then I was finding most things highly hilarious anyway. I'm a terribly giddy drunk, I feel sorry for anyone who has to put up with me when I'm mortal especially during one of my stupid laughing fits, usually over things that no one else finds the least bit funny.

Anyway, after half an hour or so of trading insults it was obvious we fancied the arse off each other and so we did the swapping phone numbers thing.

An ex rugby player, standing six foot six to my short arsed five four and almost as broad, Danny was a big, no, a huge guy in most places but as it turned out, disappointingly below average in others. Friends would often ask whether he was proportional in all areas when I was with him so let's just take a moment here to talk about penis size shall we?

Is it important? Does it matter? Well it doesn't have to be a huge chopper - too big can be uncomfortable, even painful after all and there is a lot of truth to it's not what you have it's what you do with it that counts, but to be brutally honest it does help if you can actually feel it. Asking "Is it in yet?" can kind of ruin the moment. Not that Danny's was that small mind you, but sadly no, it definitely was not in proportion to the rest of him. You know what they say about men with big feet? Yeah - they wear big shoes. Trust me I've done extensive research on the subject and the size of a guy's manhood does not correlate to the size of his feet nor to the size of his thumbs either for that matter. It's a fallacy. So no, 6ft 6, size 14 feet, hands like shovels does not necessarily equate to 10 inches of chunky prime man meat.

Back to the pub, I was thoroughly enjoying myself chatting and flirting with Danny but all too soon it was time to leave. It was still quite early but I was out with my friends on a girls night and we were going on to a club. We were all a bit skint it being almost two weeks until payday so the plan was to see if we could score a free bottle or two of fake Champagne (that awful, cheap fizzy cider crap that gives you a bastard of a hangover) by pretending it was someone's birthday and then dance around our handbags like disco divas studiously ignoring all unworthy male attention. As it was a girlie night I wasn't allowed to invite Danny along so we said our goodbyes after we swapped numbers, had a long lingering snog which further awakened the delicious feelings in my loins, and off we went on our, by then very merry, separate ways.

CHAPTER 5

I t was about five weeks later before Danny actually called me and I'd almost forgotten about our encounter which, to be quite honest, was a little hazy to begin with after the amount of alcohol that had been consumed that night. I was thinking he mustn't be very interested in me after all so I had put him out of my mind. His excuse for taking so long to contact me? Well he had managed to get himself arrested for drunken brawling shortly after we had met that night in the pub and was being prosecuted. Apparently the law takes none too kindly toward you giving someone a good smack and requires that you are suitably punished for such bad deeds. He wasn't sure I'd want to see him under the circumstances but I said I didn't mind, agreeing we all had occasional lapses in judgement, especially when a little drunk and yes the other guy probably had deserved it. To be honest, I didn't really care, I'd fancied him (even though I couldn't actually recall what he looked liked, just that he'd given me fanny flutters) and I just wanted a shag. It had been a while.

I agreed to meet him for a date and so we

met up a couple of days later at a bar situated at Piccadilly train station. It happened to be St Georges day. This saint thing was becoming a bit of a theme, an ironic one given the circumstances of Danny's conception. Now the English are a bit more of a reserved lot than the Irish so instead of getting arseholed on pints of mild, wearing silly hats, tearfully singing Jerusalem or Land of Hope and Glory, Morris dancing in the streets and such carry on, people were just going about their day as normal. In fact, if it wasn't for a few desultory white flags with red crosses hanging limply from the odd shop front here and there, there would have been no nod whatsoever to this special day to commemorate the brave knight George who had heroically slain the human sacrifice demanding dragon or so the story goes. Obviously the banishment of snakes as per St Patrick, who actually wasn't even Irish, is a much more deserving cause for celebration. Or, if you're a bit cynical, a clever marketing ploy by Irish breweries.

I was stone cold sober but Danny, who obviously embraced and celebrated his English heritage as enthusiastically as his Irish, was already totally arseholed when I turned up. Slurring his words, hardly able to stand up straight, eyes pointing all different ways. I should have ran, very quickly in the opposite direction and I still to this day have no idea why I didn't, it would have saved me a whole lot of years of heartache that's for sure. Not very impressed at the pissed up state he was in but reluctant to go home and leave him for some strange reason I have never figured out, I suggested we go to a nearby cafe with the hopes of sobering him up a little. After eating enough food to feed about seventeen normal people and leaving me to foot the bill, he did appear to sober up, at least enough to hold a bit of a conversation. We talked about the usual romantic first date stuff - anal sex, drinking, fighting, getting arrested, and his favourite hobby, football hooliganism. Oh and he flirted shamelessly with every woman under the age of fifty that walked by and tried to start a fight with at least half a dozen men. As first dates go it was certainly very memorable. I caught the train home after a couple of hours not sure I wanted to see him again but he was quite aggressive in his pursuit of me and managed to persuade me to go on another date with him. He promised he wouldn't get so drunk this time.

We ended up having a lunch date a few days later which really wasn't any better. Yes, he was pissed once again and we got kicked out of my favourite Italian restaurant because he had an altercation with one of the waiters. Seeing that he was a little worse for wear the waiter refused to serve him any more alcohol. Danny kept shouting "I want a fucking beer! Do you know who I am? Do you?! Stuck up bastard!".

Erm, no Danny all he knew was that you were a big, drunken arsehole. It was so embarrassing, everyone staring and tutting and shaking their heads. I apologised profusely to the angry staff and we ended up going back to my house still hungry. I was too ashamed to ever show my face in that particular restaurant ever again.

That was our first night together, well late afternoon really as he was on bail, under curfew and had to back at his parents for 7pm. It wasn't anything special. The sex was a bit rubbish. Him being drunk (a state he obviously favoured those days) had an unfavourable impact on his performance. It took some coaxing to get his dick to stand to attention and then it only lasted a minute or so anyway. An awful lot of effort for not a lot in return. It wasn't exactly very romantic either. Afterwards he looked deep into my eyes, said "D'ya know, ya have verr borinair an yer a bit fat" then fell into a snoring, farting, drunken slumber, drooling all over my pillows and mumbling about "fucking stuck up bastards" whilst I lay there next to him, arms crossed, glaring at the ceiling frustrated, shooting occasional angry looks at him and barely resisting the urge to give him a couple of good hard kicks or elbows to the head.

Well he was definitely a keeper this one for sure right? Quite a catch. Overly fond of the drink, loved a fight, criminal record, unemployed, skint, living with his parents, womaniser, on bail with a 7pm curfew and if all that wasn't bad enough he had the ugliest feet I have ever seen and he was in serious need of a bloody good wash. His armpits were rather wiffy and the rest of him wasn't too pleasantly fragrant either. But despite all this I started to see him on a regular basis.

Why??

Mostly I think because he wouldn't take no for an answer and he could be very charming when he wanted to be. He was always very apologetic about his drunken behaviour and constantly made promises to clean up his act. Sure OK, occasionally he was sober and he even took a shower from time to time but I still to this day have absolutely no idea what on earth I saw in him. Had I really been that desperate for a boyfriend and a bit of shit sex?

They say love is blind, in this case I think I took leave of all five of my senses. I blame pheromones, sneaky little bastards that they are, making me fall for this specimen of exactly what not to look for in a man. With the exception of a few short lived and not at all serious flings I had been happily single for the best part of five years, then I go and fall for Mr Totally Wrong.

In all fairness, after a few false starts, he did manage to calm down somewhat and grow up a bit once we had been an item for a few months. I'd finally given him an ultimatum after one particular messy time when he'd gone to watch football at lunchtime promising not to drink and to be at mine by 6pm so we could go out for a meal. He'd finally turned up at 3am the next morning so pissed up he'd pissed himself in the taxi and I'd had to give the driver £60 to get the seat cleaned. I was utterly sick of the drinking by this point and I told him in no uncertain terms to clean up his act or bugger off.

To my surprise he did clean up, a little anyway. He received a suspended sentence and community service for his earlier misdemeanor, stopped getting into trouble with the law, mostly knocked the drinking on the head and finally even managed to get himself a steady job. He never did quite get the hang of regular showers though and sadly there was nothing to be done about the seriously ugly feet apart from amputation which would have been a little extreme I suppose. He was still lazy though, aggressive, let me pay for everything and could start an argument about nothing just for the fun of it.

The relationship lasted just shy of ten years and I think I actually liked him for maybe four of those, perhaps even loved him at times, well at least during those times he wasn't driving me to despair and insanity. He asked me to marry him several times. He even bought me a ring, which was really beautiful and which he presented to me inside a cracker in what was nearly quite a romantic Christmas dinner proposal. Only slightly spoiled by a huge argument about who was doing the washing up which ended up with me throwing all the crockery out into the yard in temper and smashing it to smithereens screaming "Well no one needs to fucking wash it now do they?!" much to the amusement of the horrible nosey bitch who lived next door to me and just happened to be stood out in her yard probably so she could hear what was going on better.

Danny always had that effect on me, turning me into a crazy woman who wanted to break things, usually over his head, and scream after spending any significant amount of time with him. I'd been married once and doing it again never really appealed to me, at least not with Danny, and I'm so glad we never got around to it and will be eternally grateful that we never produced a child.

I know you are probably thinking why on earth did she stay with him for so long? I often ask myself the same thing. The sex was OK at first but it was nothing spectacular so it wasn't that. He never had any money, wasn't particularly good company, was a miserable, unsociable bugger. Why do people stay in relationships for years on end when they are obviously unhappy? Why do we put up with awful behaviour, violence, infidelity, lies, abuse? Is it just a habitual thing? A fear of being alone? Financial concerns, kids, fear of failure? Scared of change? A combination of all of these things maybe? I do know this for sure though now - life is far too short to be unhappy but when do you know it's time to get out, that it's pointless wasting any more of your time on a relationship that is going nowhere?

In this case, the decision was made for me

when I discovered he was cheating on me. I was a bit angry of course when I found out. OK more like fucking furious. For reasons beyond my comprehension I had invested years of my life and suffered lots of heartbreak with this idiot trying to straighten him out and he repaid me by cheating on me at one of the times of my life when I most needed some support back from him. But do you know what? Although the timing could have been better, whoever you are lady I soon came to realise that you actually did me a massive favour and I thank you. You are more than welcome to the narcissistic, lazy, tight fisted, smelly, argumentative, miserable arse and his seriously ugly feet. I wish you well, you are going to need all the luck you can get.

So there I was, back to square one, only this time I was in my 40's. Fat, skint and single once again. Finding a new man was going to be a bit more of a challenge this time around.

CHAPTER 6

*"It was a slap in the face, how quickly I was replaced.
And are you thinking of me when you fuck her?"*

YOU OUGHTA KNOW - ALANIS MORISSETTE 1995

F inding myself single again after so long was a bit of a shock to the system. I was alternatively giddy with freedom and relief, then overwhelmed with anxiety, sadness and loneliness. There was also a large element of jealousy and humiliation to deal with after the way it ended so I was mostly raging with anger. I was positively seething in the early days, totally unreasonable, I just wanted to shout and throw things which was nothing new when it came to Danny. He had cheated on me after all, with the worst possible timing and let's face it no one likes to be cheated on. How dare he, the bastard!

However, my breakup couldn't really be classed as a tragedy and I soon accepted it was actually a blessing, freeing me from a very unhappy and unfulfilling relationship, but I still went through a sort of grieving process. I was not grieving for the loss of the delightful Danny though no, I think it was more for the decade of my life, the prime years I had wasted on trying to salvage such a shit relationship. Why oh why? There was no point in worrying about that though, I couldn't change it, couldn't get that part of my life back. I just needed to learn to focus on moving forward and enjoying my life from now onwards. Regret, like jealousy and anger, really is a pointless waste of time and energy but it is hard to control what you are feeling sometimes.

Then, as if all the mad, uncontrollable emotions weren't enough to cope with, there was the massive upheaval to the practical side of my life. I had left him but had nowhere to live. I had no parents to go and stay with as they had both passed away and there was no room to stay with my daughter as she and her boyfriend lived in the tiniest apartment in the world. Because they lived in the city centre they paid an astronomical amount of rent for the privilege of residing in a minuscule place which boasted a tiny combined living room / kitchen / bedroom with a separate bathroom all crammed into about 60 square feet. City centre living. I had seen bigger garden sheds.

Never being very good at adulting I had no savings to speak of so whilst I desperately tried to beg, borrow and scrape the money together for the extortionate fees I needed so I could rent my own place me, and Walter my old ginger tomcat, ended up staying with my friend Alice for a while. Lovely Alice was now was a single mum to two young boys after a failed marriage to a selfish fuckwit who couldn't keep his dick in his pants when he was working away from home. She generously offered me the use of her spare room for however long I needed it. It was the smallest bedroom you could ever imagine, you could lie in the single bed, open your arms and literally touch the walls on either side of the room, very claustrophobic, but beggars can't be choosers and I was very grateful for her letting me stay there, a much better alternative to sleeping on the streets that's for sure.

After five or six weeks at Alice's our friendship was becoming a little strained, her two unbelievably noisy, messy, hyperactive nine and eleven year old monsters were testing my patience daily and working from home I had no escape. Why don't kids bugger off out to play any more? All they do is play video games and watch crap on YouTube. I have no idea how she put up with the ungrateful, argumentative little shits every day without resorting to duct taping their mouths closed, handcuffing them and locking them in the cupboard under the stairs.

"Where on earth do your boys get all their energy from?" I asked as we relaxed with a well deserved bottle of Chardonnay one evening after a particularly trying day with the little monsters.

"I'm pretty damn sure they suck it directly from my soul" answered Alice taking a large gulp of wine.

I certainly had a new found respect for her and how she dealt with the constant, loud and exhausting solo shitstorm her life had become since she'd kicked her husband out, still managing to hold down a responsible and very stressful full time job and parenting single without going completely insane. I did have some concerns about the amount of alcohol she consumed every evening but I suppose she needed something to help get her through.

I longed for peace and quiet and a child free environment but because I had my cat it took a couple of months to find somewhere of my own. It was ridiculously difficult to find a landlord that accepted pets even though Walter was so fat and old and lazy the only damage he ever did was to his food. I did eventually find a furnished tiny cottage in a little village about ten miles away. It was sitting in an overgrown jungle of a garden, was damp, drab and dingy and smelt like someone had died in there (they probably had). It was in desperate need of cleaning and decorating but it was within my budget and I managed to negotiate a fairly decent drop in the first year's rent and deposit in return for promising to decorate the house and tidy up the garden a bit. Whilst I would be eternally grateful to Alice for saving me and my furball from being homeless we were both nonetheless relieved to move into our own place.

Once settled in the cottage with nothing

but work to occupy my mind and no noisy, hyper, horrible kids to distract me, I started to go through the usual stages of getting over a breakup. The rites of passage back to singledom. In my case this consisted mostly of drinking copious amounts of booze, scoffing several tons of chocolate, getting through a freezer full of ice cream and a good few boxes of tissues. I also shouted along angrily, usually at around 2am and after a bottle of wine, to Alanis Morrisette's "You Oughta Know" on repeat, full blast. It's a good, shouty, angry song. If two bottles of wine had been demolished, you would probably have found me crying and badly singing some soppy love shit to an unimpressed Walter instead who would sit looking at me for a minute or so with a totally unfathomable expression on his ginger whiskery face before darting off to hide somewhere quiet where he could give his poor ears a rest from the tuneless onslaught.

My new neighbours must have absolutely loved me, especially as I am a bit on the deaf side meaning my full volume is a bit louder than the norm and my singing is dire at the best of times never mind when I am drunk. But hey, their dogs bark incessantly when they're out so I'll just consider it advance payback.

Of course, we had the time honored tradition of trashing the ex with your best buddies, to which all my lovely friends contributed with great enthusiasm. It's amazing how none of them had

ever liked him anyway. Coming up with inventive new insulting names for him was great fun,
cheering me up no end. Then of course let us not
forget the "Let's Make a Complete Tit of Yourself"
stage which can run concurrently with all the
others.

I wish I could say that I am a mature, well bal-
anced adult and I completely bypassed this one
but to my shame I did embarrass myself a time
or two. Mostly by playing drunk Text the Ex Rou-
lette. For those few of you not in the know this
consists of sending messages to your ex via text,
WhatsApp, Facebook - oh so many lovely messaging mediums to choose from - whilst under the
influence of several alcoholic beverages.

These messages can range from you pleading
to get back together because you love and miss
him (you don't, you're just pissed and lonely and
probably horny) or my favourite which was telling him how much you hate him and you wish
he'd just fuck off and die with imaginative and
painful suggestions of just exactly how he could
go and do that. You would also usually chuck in
a couple of insults regarding his sexual performance and some derogatory comments about the
size of his manhood occasionally too just for a bit
of variety.

The fun with this game is that you never know
which way it's going to go until you start to
type. Nothing makes your heart sink faster than
waking up the next day with a whopping hang-

over and alcohol induced memory loss to discover you have been messaging your ex whilst you were pissed. Saving their number as "That Fucking Wanker" or "Cheating Cockwomble" or some other such loving term of endearment will not prevent you from doing this. The best thing is to remove his contact information completely from your phone before starting on the demon drink, it will save you from tons of embarrassment later. If you discover you have messaged, whatever you do, do not read them nor any replies he has sent. Just delete them straight away and pretend like it didn't happen. You can't be held accountable for the actions of drunken you. Well, that is as long as you don't actually carry out any of the imaginative and painful ways to help him to die in which case I've been assured by a solicitor friend of mine being drunk would not be an acceptable defence. Please note, criminal damage is unlikely to be excused either so it's not a good idea to take your anger out on his car or other personal possessions.

Please, please, please, do not have sex with your ex under any circumstances. Especially whilst drunk. No matter how lonely or desperate you get, it's always a very, very, very bad idea. It will put you back weeks. Luckily this time Danny had already moved on and moved her, the slapper from work who obviously had no morals, into our old place with breathtaking speed. That's not to say I didn't consider it, I even got a taxi over once after a shit night out when I was feeling especially lonely (this was how I discovered he'd moved her in). It was just very painful, embarrassing and uncomfortable for us both, probably for her too, me turning up unannounced to find her there in my bed. But it stopped me from potentially making a big mistake which I was thankful for when I managed to get a grip and regain my senses. Twice in the past I'd had misguided drunken sex with ex's. It didn't end well either time.

How long does it take to get over someone? As they say, how long is a piece of string? It is impossible to put a timeline on it. It could take days, weeks, months, even years. In some very tragic cases people even occasionally die from broken hearts. Sometimes you just need a bottle of wine or two and a good long soak in a hot bubble bath. Sometimes you will need a good therapist, prescription drugs and maybe some anger management sessions. Sometimes it's a gradual thing the loss, anger and sadness ebbing away over time. Sometimes you just wake up one day, feeling different not sure why at first then realising he's no longer taking up any head space and think "I'm over it, thank fuck for that!"

How and when it does happen it's such a relief. Your stomach will stop lurching when you think of him, you stop checking your phone every two minutes hoping for a message from him, your heart doesn't race every time you see or hear or smell something that reminds you of him. That awful anxiety and sadness and anger that has been weighing you down disappears and you simply just don't care about them anymore. It's the best feeling ever. You stop longing for them and missing them and start to wonder what on earth you actually saw in them. Your heart has healed, you're wonderfully free and ready to move on.

Thankfully I was able to get over my breakup fairly quickly. Not too many tears were wasted on the sad fucker that had been ruining my life for over a decade. After a few short weeks I gave myself a kick up the arse, deleted Greatest Love Songs and Jagged Little Pill off my playlist (no doubt much to the relief of Walter and my long suffering neighbours) then started to embrace the upsides to my newly found single status.

For example, I have terrible insomnia and crave the strangest of foods in the early hours when everyone else is sleeping so I could now eat crisp butties or pickled onions in the lovely big bed that I had all to myself at 2am if I wanted to. I could have coco pops or toast for my tea instead of having to cook a meal every night for an ungrateful bastard, be in control of the TV remote, play whatever music I wanted to as loudly as I wanted to in the car which now always had diesel in the tank. There were no dirty socks stuffed down the back of the sofa, nobody put empty milk cartons back in the fridge, the toilet seat stayed down and I didn't have to run upstairs to check for skid-marks and discarded dirty under-crackers before a visitor used the loo. But best of all, the only person I had to argue with was the cat who never took me on anyway. I hadn't realised just how much negative energy the constant arguing produced, it had been exhausting. Oh and did I mention the lovely big bed that didn't smell of sweaty unwashed man that I now had all to myself?

On the whole I was happy, but sometimes I got bored or lonely and more than occasionally horny. I always did have a high sex drive. I decided that maybe it was time to get back out there and start looking for someone new. I didn't want love, wasn't ready for that yet but someone to shag occasionally would be nice. Yes, dinner, drinks and a bit of a tumble between the sheets once or twice a week with a decent guy would be just perfect.

CHAPTER 7

Where on earth do you start to look for new love or even just a bit of no strings attached fun? Apparently a lot of people meet their partners at work but when you work from home, your options are rather limited. Pubs and clubs maybe but unless you're lucky enough to have a nice local where you can actually get to know people they are such an artificial environment. Everyone is scrubbed up and dressed in their best clobber, happy, drunk and determined to have a good time. Although a lot of people do meet this way - inebriated, giddy, full of Dutch courage and wearing beer goggles, it's probably not the best condition to be in when looking for a new relationship.

So to my first girl's night out on the town as a singleton and on the pull. There I was, a bit of a fatty, past my prime but dressed to impress and full of vodka induced confidence. I hadn't drunk much whilst I was in my last relationship, actually hadn't gotten out all that much. He was an unsociable arse and sulked like a child if I went out with my friends so I didn't used to bother all that often, just wasn't worth the hassle. But happily I discovered binge drinking was just like riding a bike, once learned never forgotten and I soon got the hang of it again. It's something I'd always been quite good at - social masochism. I appear to have a natural gift for getting stupidly pissed and making a complete dick of myself in public.

I stood at the bar and surreptitiously eyed up the available talent which was a little sparse but there were a couple of possibilities. I can get a man of course I can, just watch me!

Oh dear.

What is it about alcohol that can turn even the most shy introvert into an outrageous flirt? One minute I was feeling maybe a little tipsy, worrying if I was too old and fat for the length of my skirt, concerned that it may be revealing a few too many thigh dimples. One tiny, little shot of vodka later and there I was, utterly convinced that I was a devastatingly attractive sex Goddess - just call me Venus! I was under the impression that I was totally irresistible and that everybody wanted me. Fuck my fat legs and never mind that chubby belly, just look at my amazing tits! I was unashamedly, lasciviously licking my lips, suggestively sucking my straw and making wanton eye contact with anyone who took my fancy. My beer goggles were firmly in place by that point so pretty much any male under sixty with a pulse was looking like fair game.

After an outrageously terrible karaoke perform-ance of Gloria Gaynor's "I Will Survive" (I'm also under the very mistaken impression that I'm an awesome singer when I've had a few) I got flirting with someone. Male, tick, right age bracket, tick, not totally repulsive, tick, able to string a sen-tence together, tick. Even though I was consider-ably out of practice I thought all was going rather well. That was at least until I fell over and landed unceremoniously on my arse. Luckily, as it was well upholstered at the time the only thing that was bruised was my pride. After hefting me back up on to my unsteady feet, not an easy task given my weight and being totally plastered, I think he mumbled something about going to the loo and then he vanished never to be seen again.

Probably a good thing. Given that I seemed to have lost all coordination and even standing up-right was beyond my capabilities by that point I think shagging or at least my active partici-pation in the act would have been completely out of the question. Maybe I'd had just a little too much vodka or perhaps someone spiked my drink I suggested to my friends as they laughingly poured me into a taxi and sent me home.

I am blessed, or cursed depending on what kind of mood I'm in, with large breasts. Great for flirting, bad for fitted dresses, sleeping on your stomach or going on those funfair rides that have the sort of safety harness things that clamp down over your chest painfully flattening your breasticles. Obviously designed by a man or a flat chested woman with severe boob envy. Summer underboob sweat isn't too delightful or sexy either, as for taking up jogging to keep fit, forget it, even the most sturdy of sports bras fail to keep oversized knockers in their place.

A lot of men go gaga for big bouncy fun bags, drooling over those voluptuous mounds of fat that nature kindly gave us to feed babies with. When faced with a nice pair some men appear to suffer from the phenomenon known as Mammary Loss. This condition makes them forget things, for example - having a significant other at home, how rude it is to stare, especially with your tongue hanging out, or simply just how to behave in a respectful manner. Just because we are showing off a bit of cleavage boys does not mean you have the right to touch. Calm down, pop your eyes and tongue back in and kindly keep your dirty paws to yourselves unless otherwise invited.

I considered my boobs to be one of my best assets and they certainly got a lot of attention whilst I was out, which on the whole was great as it took the eye away from my fat stomach and enormous bingo wings. There were downsides too. One night I got chatting to a guy I thought was reasonably good looking and rather lovely. That was until he asked me if I would hold his pint whilst he went to the loo, thinking himself oh so hilarious, witty and clever when he inserted it in-between my boobs which were hoisted up to their best advantage in a super-strong push-up bra invitingly spilling out from a sparkly revealing top, black of course. He didn't appear to find it so funny when I removed his drink from my cleavage and poured it over his stupid head. Neither did the bouncers who escorted me out of the club, but excuse me who's actually in the wrong here? If he'd have been famous I probably could have cried to the press and sued him for sexual harrasment.

CHAPTER 8

Anyway, after a few nights out, drunkenly and shamelessly throwing myself at anyone I found attractive but going home alone, I did finally get lucky. Hands up if you've ever given your number to someone or even worse, woken up with someone you found gorgeous and hilariously entertaining when under the influence the night before who actually looks and smells like an Orc on a bad day with the personality of a dead fish the next morning once you have sobered up. Yep. Like that it was. Bloody beer goggles.

Drunken one night stands, such a very bad idea. I went home with this guy, can't even remember the sex if we had any it must have been very boring. I do recall gobbling his man lolly with great gusto and then gagging and almost upchucking my six double vodka Red Bulls and the dodgy chicken kebab I'd eaten on the way home when he started to ejaculate into my mouth. Doing an impression of a cat choking on a hairball with semen running down your chin isn't the least bit sexy I can assure you. I don't recall what happened next, maybe I'd passed out due to a lack of oxygen whilst I was choking.

So, I'd either passed out or fallen into a drunken coma and my punishment was that I had to go through the awful, mortifying waking up with a stranger who's seen you naked scenario the next morning. Best to disappear into the night like a mysterious nymph than wake up next to someone who's name you can't even remember. Being in a strange bed with a strange man, naked, sober, hungover and tormented with flashbacks of throwing off your clothes with wild abandon and making ridiculous porn star worthy dirty talk the night before isn't a great way to start your day. It got better.

I was really, really desperate for a pee, like at that point where you are almost crying with the need for relief. I also needed to fart but dared not even try to sneak out a little one as the aforementioned dodgy chicken kebab was making some very strange and violent moves through my digestive system. My bowels were bubbling like a witches cauldron and any attempt to discreetly pass wind would have most likely ended up a messy shart.

I needed a gallon of water, my mouth was like sandpaper, and I had breath that would have wilted the hardiest of plants, maybe even killed small creatures if they had been unfortunate enough for me to breathe on them. I was painfully aware of the things I hadn't cared about when drunk - cellulite, saggy tits, stretch marks, wobbly belly, wrinkles. It was bright and sunny in the bedroom, no hiding in the dark. I knew I would look deranged, makeup smeared all over my face and the pillow. My hair resembling an abandoned bird's nest. This is a mystery to me, I have the finest, lankest, straightest hair which refuses any and all attempts at introducing volume when I'm trying, however after a night out I wake up and it has transformed into something that resembles a permed, back-combed and hair-sprayed to death horror from the 80's.

 I lay there in the strange man's bed not daring to move, pretending I was asleep, praying he, whoever he was, would bugger off to the loo before my bladder exploded and I pissed his bed. This wasn't beyond the realms of possibility given the fact that I'd had a child and as I'd been criminally lackadaisical regarding pelvic floor exercises (in fact all exercise) my bladder control wasn't what it used to be. Just one small sneeze at that moment in time could have resulted in disastrous consequences either wet, loud or messy. Or even all three at the same time. I was starting to panic, wondering if he was also pretending to be asleep so he didn't need to acknowledge my presence. Maybe he was hoping I would just get up and leave so he wouldn't have to talk to me. That was fine by me I thought as I peeped through one eye frantically trying to locate my clothes so I could dive out of bed Ninja style and throw them on in record time. I had just spied the location of my bra and was formulating my escape plan when finally, hallelujah! he stirred, stretched and got up out of bed.

I concentrated very hard on pretending to be asleep until I heard him leave the room (how hard is it to do that fake deep, even breathing thing?) As soon as I was sure it was all clear I jumped up and got dressed super quick with my legs crossed and my arse clenched which I can tell you requires great skill and balance especially when suffering from the hangover from hell.

He came back into the bedroom a few minutes later, we exchanged hesitant half smiles with minimal eye contact and finally I escaped, making my way to the toilet. Ah sweet relief as I pissed about four gallons. That letting go when you've been so desperate to go for ages is almost better than an orgasm, but then oh no! The guts wanted rid too.

Like many British people, I have a phobia about pooing on a toilet that isn't mine. I'd had intimate relations with this man but was reluctant to have a number two on his toilet. We all have to do it so why is it considered such a taboo and embarrassing thing to do? And why does it have to smell so bad?

It was the smallest toilet room in the world, he had no air freshener, I couldn't open the window, it was somehow stuck and I was worried about the no doubt loud and questionable noises, not to mention the awful smell that the dodgy chicken kebab evacuation would make. However my choices were a: use his toilet or b: soil myself. It had to be done.

After what felt like about three hours my guts finally stopped trying to turn themselves inside out but to my horror there were only about four squares of very cheap toilet paper which fell woefully short of what was required for the cleanup operation and I couldn't find anymore. I was shuffling around, very unladylike with my knickers around my ankles desperately looking for something to clean myself with, but there was nothing that I could use, not even an old sponge or a newspaper. There wasn't even any soap on the tiny hand basin. There was nothing for it, the knickers had to be sacrificed.

I managed to clean myself but then was at a loss with what to do with the soiled, soggy undergarment. I had the smallest handbag with me, not much bigger than a coin purse. These were size 18, firm control, big belly warmers with reinforced gusset, proper passion killers, they weren't for fitting in the teeny, tiny bag. I contemplated throwing them out of the window into the neighbours garden but then remembered the bloody thing wouldn't open. I had no other option, down the loo they had to go. I tried to rip them into smaller pieces but they were made of some super indestructible, extra stretchy material which was impossible to tear.

Six flushes and some brutal encouragement from the bog brush it took for Primark's finest full control briefs to finally disappear around the u bend. He must have been wondering why I flushed his loo so many times, certainly didn't look very impressed when I shamefully scuttled back into the bedroom, my face burning with embarrassment. Maybe he was on a water meter and a tight budget.

I followed him downstairs to his kitchen and we made very awkward conversation for about five seconds.

"Are you OK?" he asked the wall behind me studiously avoiding eye contact.

"Yes. Thank you. I'm Good. Thanks for asking." I replied to his fridge.

"Errr... Good. That's Good. OK then. Errr... Would you like me to give you a lift home?" He asked the kettle.

"Oh, no. Thanks for offering, but you're probably still over the limit. Haha! I'll order a taxi. But thank you." I was already tapping the taxi number into my mobile. The thought of being in such close proximity to him in a car was just too much to cope with.

"Ah, yeah. Good point." He said to the floor, visibly relieved "Errr. OK. Mmmm... Would you er, like erm, a coffee?"

I declined, eager to escape before the foul smell I had made in the toilet sneaked under the door and permeated the rest of the house.

Luckily the taxi arrived fairly quickly and we parted with an almost audible sigh of relief, for both of us I'm sure. No numbers were exchanged, no "Well! This was fun shall we do it again?" No lingering kisses. A muttered "Er... See ya then" whilst looking at the floor was as good as it got.

It was a chilly morning and outside in the cold light of day the dress I felt so sexy in the night before along with the fact that I was commando made me feel like a right dirty old trollop. The taxi driver smirked at me knowingly in the rear view mirror all the way home. "Keep your eyes on the road" I growled at him.

I was very tempted to flash my naked, fat arse at the judgemental bastard when we arrived at my house. I painfully peeled my bare, sweaty thighs off the leather seats, leaving a layer of skin behind and got out of the car then completed the walk of shame up my garden path under the watchful eye of the miserable old bat who lived directly opposite me. No doubt she was full of disgusted delight at my disheveled state and would be fairly bursting to relay this information to the league of jam making ladies at the church. I could hear her tuts of disapproval through her sparkling clean double glazed, flowery curtained window. I barely contained the urge to give her a full moon and a double middle finger salute.

CHAPTER 9

A couple of weeks later, not letting the previous disastrous experience put me off, I was out on the prowl once more. I was a little nervous about bumping into the one night stand guy again, worried in case he presented me with an enormous bill because he had to get a plumber out to unblock his toilet, but, to my relief I didn't see him. However, after a couple more disastrous drunken nights out, I eventually came to the conclusion that the whole trying to meet someone whilst out on the piss thing was proving to be a waste of time.

I had spent a good twenty minutes in a bar one night generously allowing an old man to engage me in conversation but not really taking much notice of him because I was eyeing up his cute mate. Cute mate followed me when I excused myself and tottered off over to the bar in my ridiculously uncomfortable, stupidly high heels, swinging my hips, sticking out my ample chest whilst trying to suck in my ample stomach. In my deluded mind I thought I was walking with a sexy swagger when in reality it probably looked more like a comedy six vodka stagger.

At the bar the cute mate approached me, smiled shyly and said "Hi, I hope you don't mind me saying, you're very pretty"

I smiled back and fluttered my false eyelashes at him, my vodka fuelled ego growing unchecked. "Thank you" I replied. He really was very good looking, a bit on the young side maybe but mmmm.

"Are you single?" He enquired

"Yes, as it happens." I said sipping at my drink in a coquettish manner and silently thinking to myself "I've still got it. Game on!"

"Great, can I take your number?" he asked. Then, nodding over at the guy I had been chatting with "You seemed to get on really well with my dad. He really fancies you but he's too shy to do anything about it and he's been really lonely since my mum left him. He's only 42, he needs a new woman in his life."

His what? His bloody DAD?! I almost spat my mouthful of vodka and lime all over him. My inflated ego popped like a balloon. Mortified, I squinted at him. Now he was in focus and I could see him properly he was actually very, very, young. Like barely out of his teens type young. His beard made him look older. When did boys under 25 start to grow beards? I really needed to go get my eyes tested and get some new contact lenses. And stop thinking I was only 24. I was then further horrified when the realisation of something he'd said hit me. His dad was 42, the "old" man I'd been obligingly chatting to was actually a year younger than me. Jesus Christ.

My face flamed with embarrassment. What was I thinking? I was too old for this! I should be sat at home on a Saturday night wearing a cardigan and fluffy slipper socks, contently married to a boring but safe and predictable man called Bob or Malcom. Watching period dramas and the news every evening together sat on the sofa in companionable silence broken only by the occasional comment on world affairs or asking "would you like another cup of tea love?"

Happily finding my thrills and excitement in knitting or making découpage whatever the hell that was. Having scheduled, silent, unsatisfactory sex in the same position once a month with the lights out whilst fantasizing about Simon Cowell. Calling each other "Love" and saying "love you" without even thinking about it. Growing old gracefully. But no, here I was, making a complete tit of myself getting stupidly drunk every weekend, thinking I was twenty years younger than I really was and perversely lusting over boys who probably hadn't even been born in the same millennium as me. Oh God, I was going to turn into Millie Mayor.

Millie was a neighbour from my childhood. A sex mad, ancient old lady who lived a few doors down from my parents, a real character. She was completely and utterly bonkers and would sit in her front garden in the summer, off her face on Harvey's Bristol Cream, face badly made up with heaps of blue sparkly eyeshadow, very pink cheeks and smudged bright red lipstick. Her usual outfit was a leather mini skirt, stripper heels and various cropped, see-through tops with no underwear. Rumour had it she'd been a very beautiful woman in her day. Apparently she had been the not so secret lover of some local rich fella who had steadfastly refused to leave his wife for her. Millie had eventually gone a bit mental with all the fruitless waiting and hoping that he would leave his wife and make an honest woman of her. Another, more popular and colourful rumour was that she had been a highly paid prostitute. Very kinky, talented with a whip and extremely popular with members of parliament and rich, powerful business leaders.

When I think back I realise Millie was obviously mentally unwell. Possibly suffering with dementia. She probably would have been put in some care facility these days or locked up for lewd behaviour but she had been harmless enough. Her thing would be to flash her droopy boobs at the local boys when they rode past on their bikes and invite them in for a custard slice. She had no modesty or shame. 'Custard slice" became the neighbourhood slang for a shag. As far as I know no one ever took her up on this offer but I can never hear the words "custard slice" without thinking first of sex then secondly (and disturbingly) of poor Millie's sad, old, deflated boobs which hung like a basset hound's ears with her nipples poking out of the bottom of her cropped top.

I decided I had to stop this going out on the pull nonsense. I was just making a complete and utter idiot of myself. Although I had met Danny this way (and look how that turned out) the reality was that I was very unlikely to meet someone for a meaningful relationship pissed up in a busy bar. The best I could hope for was a brief fumbled encounter with a fellow pisshead and I really didn't fancy spending my life lurching from one drunken one night stand to another. In all honesty the one I'd had hadn't been any fun, quite soul destroying in fact and let's face it, drunken sex, even when you can remember it, is usually mediocre at best. They either can't get an erection, come in seconds then fall into a drunken, snoring, farting coma or pound you for hours until you are sober again, your fanny is raw and you are begging for mercy and sleep. No, I got way more satisfaction with far less effort or worry of potential embarrassment or sexually transmitted disease from my Rampant Rabbit so I invested in some rechargeable batteries. But I did sometimes miss kisses and cuddles and that human connection, the ordinary, everyday things that you take for granted when you're in a relationship and miss so much when you're single. Just someone to say "How was your day honey?" and take away that loneliness I sometimes felt in an evening when my work was done for the day would be lovely. The rabbit was great at giving orgasms but pretty shit at conversation and no good for hugs.

Friends sympathised and told me not to worry, assuring me that I would meet someone when I was least expecting it. But living in a rather rural area and working from home I could often go days without seeing anyone apart from the post-man who was a: female and b: about 64 years old. The local pub was full of the same old faces all the time, old being the key word here, the average age of my village being around 74 the usual relationship status either widowed or fifty plus years married. You were more likely to find a hen with teeth than a single, straight man under the age of fifty within a five mile radius of where I lived.

I read an article in a magazine about the super-market being a good hunting ground for potential partners so I gave that a try for a while. I soon got fed up though of driving ten miles to the nearest big store to linger up and down the aisles like a desperate wraith surreptitiously eyeing up all the men of a certain age trying to figure out who looked as though they could possibly be single. Those carrying baskets containing one or more of the following:- frozen microwave dinners for one, beer and porn mags were a fairly good bet.

Once or twice I sidled up to a potential singleton, smiled and tried to make friendly conversation but they would just look at me as if I had escaped from an asylum and then nervously scuttle off throwing startled looks at me over their shoulder. Being friendly to strangers in a supermarket is obviously not the done thing. After a few days of this I think the security staff were beginning to get a bit suspicious of the regularity of my visits and the ridiculous amount of time it took me to select and purchase my average of two items. They were probably also thinking I'd escaped from the local loony bin and they'd started to follow me, rather obviously, around the store. So I gave up on that idea rather quickly.

I considered changing my career to something where I would come into regular contact with lots of men, such as brick laying, but frankly couldn't be arsed so I gave community college a go. Not sure why. First an art class where the students disappointingly, mostly consisted of menopausal, depressed and depressing, married middle aged women in floaty, floral print dresses with a startling amount of chin whiskers and moustaches between them. There was one man, my age, good looking, no wedding ring, yey! A possibility until I discovered he was as gay as a lord and happily living with his partner of ten plus years who he affectionately referred to as Queen Sparkle Bottom (I never felt the need to ask him how or why his partner had been christened that) and their two princess pugs Marilyn and Kylie.

I saw a poster up on the college notice board advertising a free bicycle repair and maintenance class happening one Saturday morning so I sacrificed my usual weekend lie in and gave that a go, although under false pretences as I didn't own, nor did I ever intend to own, a bicycle and had zero interest in the subject. I did, very briefly in a brief moment of madness entertain the idea of buying one, my mind full of idyllic fantasies of being fit and slim with shapely legs from cycling down country lanes in the lovely sunshine. Then I remembered that I lived in England where it pissed it down most of the time and that I lived in a village surrounded by such steep hills that I struggled to get up them in my car never mind trying to ride a bicycle up them. Also I would look utterly ridiculous in Lycra with all my wobbly chub and then there was the fact that everyone hates cyclists.

Regardless, ever optimistic and increasingly desperate, along I trotted to find the class was made up of a couple of chubby adolescent boys who had been reluctantly dragged along with their equally chubby dads who'd probably last rode a bike two decades ago, and three very fit men of retirement age with rock hard thighs. The type who at weekends, dressed like they were competing in the Tour de France, in their wraparound shades, and aerodynamic helmets thinking they looked cool but actually looked like complete fuckwits. They blocked the roads with their cycle buddies, waving their skinny black lycra clad arses around and generally pissing motorists off everywhere. I stuck out like a sore thumb. The latter group instinctively knew I belonged to the ranks of the pissed off car drivers that beeped at them and angrily shouted "single file you bloody tossers!" out of the window when eventually able to get past them. They just didn't appreciate the frustration of being stuck behind them for five never-ending miles, going ten miles an hour on a steep, narrow, windy, country road with your knackered old car engine overheating and threatening to explode at any moment.

I tried to look interested, hiding my yawns behind my hand as the world's most boring man with the world's most boring monotone voice explained the latest exciting developments in puncture repair kits, how to locate holes in your tyres using a puddle and what to do with strange shaped spanners and uncooperative bicycle chains. The Lycra gang weren't fooled for one minute though, shooting looks of contempt towards me throughout the whole class whilst the fat tweenagers and their fatter dads just blatantly eyed up my boobs.

CHAPTER 10

It was Halloween and I was bemoaning my useless efforts at trying to find a man to my friend Jill as we got ready to go to a horror themed fancy dress party down at the local. Jill is quite simply fabulous in every aspect. Naturally and effortlessly beautiful, confident, voluptuous figure, amazing thick blonde hair, gorgeous teeth, skin, eyes - in fact gorgeous everything and the only offspring of a very wealthy eccentric couple who spoil her rotten. You want to hate her but she's so lovely and sunny and full of life you can't help but simply love her and I do, in a purely platonic way. Most people that meet her fall immediately under her spell too, she's just dazzling.

Sexually Jill likes women. She claims she discovered she was this way inclined at the age of six when a boy tried to kiss her and it made her throw up on her shiny new red patent leather Mary Jane shoes. She has a seemingly endless string of girlfriends who are as gorgeous as she is and with whom she has the most outrageous sex. Sometimes when she was telling me about what she'd been up to I secretly wished sexuality was a choice and not a given because she definitely had more fun, and more orgasms than I did. And she could borrow her girlfriends clothes, bags and makeup as a bonus.

Gorgeous Jill was looking literally horny in a devil's outfit complete with thigh-high red leather boots and pitchfork. There were going to be a few raised blood pressures at the pub that night when she walked in that was for sure.

"What are you going as - a psychiatric patient?" she questioned laughing and raising her eyebrows at me still sat in my once white but now grey scruffy old dressing gown, hair all over the place.

"I think I'll just put on an orange t-shirt and go as a pumpkin" I moaned grabbing at my flabby belly " I'm the right shape"

"Well, you are a bit of a porker these days" She agreed with a complete lack of tact in her usual straightforward manner "you should try Keto or Paleo or Slimming World or some shit. You never know, you might meet a fat man at Slimming World and fall in love whilst swapping salad recipes. You can have lots of sexercise and get skinny together. You could be the Wills and Kate of the dieting world."

"Thanks for that" I mumbled, "You know, I don't even eat that much. I don't understand why I am so bloody fat."

"When you do eat, you eat a load of crap is why.

How many of those have you had today?" she lectured nodding at the empty Frappe cup on my bedside table.

"Only one today" I lied. I'd had two. Three the day before. I was addicted to the bloody things.

"Well, they have something like 350 calories. Each." She cheerfully informed me.

Seriously? No! How? It's only iced coffee. With a bit of squirty cream that was more air than substance. And caramel sauce. I immediately Googled it. Fuck, she was right. They should come with a warning label.

I brought her up to date on the continuing lack of dates situation as I got dressed in a not very imaginative, black, shapeless witches outfit. She thought my attempts at trying to meet a man hilarious. "Bloody hell" she laughed "Just get some t-shirts printed with "Desparate for sex" printed on them! On second thoughts, don't, that'd be far too inviting for the local thigh rubbing, tooth sucking, old perverts"

"Oh haha! Funny" I said "Seriously though, I don't think I'm ever going to have sex ever again. My hymen will grow back. I'm going to die a born again virgin."

"Don't be silly." She replied "You just need to get on the internet dating sites. You'll be inundated."

"Oh I don't know - isn't that just desperation?"

"Nah. Everyone is on there these days, It's a perfectly acceptable way of meeting people. I've even used it from time to time. Just need to learn how to weed out the tossers, the scammers and the clinically insane. Give it a go, what have you got to lose? Besides, you *are* desperate."

She was right, I was desperate, what did I have to lose? Nothing. So I reluctantly agreed to go along with her suggestion. I would join the ranks of the modern love seeking singleton and, oh joy, try internet dating.

"Ace!" Exclaimed Jill with a manic grin "I will pop round tomorrow evening and we'll get you all set up on Tinder."

Ah, Tinder. You can't really get much more straightforward and simple. If you like the look of their picture, swipe right, you don't then swipe left. You both swipe right you match. You match you can then go on to message each other. Easy yes? A bit shallow? Of course it is. All I had to go on after all was how they looked on their photograph and possibly, if I was lucky and they'd bothered, a short bio. Superficial though it was I did quite like the concept. Straightforward internet dating for dummies, efficient online boyfriend shopping for the busy modern woman and none of the 'does he like me too?' guesswork of the real world.

It was so easy when you were a teenager and you could get your best mate to sidle up to someone you've got the hots for and mutter "My friend fancies you" whilst you tried to act nonchalant, standing there hiding behind your fringe, twirling your hair around your finger staring at your shoes, your face on fire but pretending you had no idea what she was doing so you could save face if he didn't fancy you back.

When you're older and trying to act a little more sophisticated and mature things get a bit more complicated. Levels of sophistication and maturity can be affected of course on the levels of alcohol consumed. Generally, one drink means being reserved, fussy and playing hard to get, but upwards of six drinks standards start to slip and it can end up being fuck it, your face doesn't make me want to vomit, I need a shag, you'll have to do.

The dating game when you're older becomes a much more difficult ballgame with more rules and potential relationships are fraught with the considerations and complications of the five S's:

Status - is he single?

Sexuality - is he straight?

Solvency - is he skint, in gainful employment?

Sobriety - is he drink / drug dependant?

and last but definitely not least;

Sanity - is he a psychopath, narcissistic not right or emotional retard?

These vitally important things don't even cross your mind when you're younger and life and people appear to be much simpler than they really are.

Bored, waiting for Jill to arrive the next afternoon I downloaded the Tinder app onto my phone, took about three hundred selfies before I was sort of happy enough with one to use as my profile picture. I can't do selfies, my arms are too short and my face just doesn't cooperate. It seems to look alright but then in the microsecond it takes between pressing the button and the camera actually taking the picture it somehow turns into the face of a gargoyle. I edited my photo a little, just softened it up a bit to play down the wrinkles and blemishes but not full on SnapChat filter, then I entered my statistics:-

Height - short arse (thank goodness for heels)
Build - chubster (but would work on it)
Eyes - green (and usually bloodshot from vodka or lack of sleep)
Hair - long, dark (and uncooperative)
Age - 43 (but still up for it)

Then I pondered what to put for my tag line...

Young at heart, cuddly lady looking for friendship that may develop into something more.

Nah, boring.

Kinky sex goddess looking for sex god to complete my life.

Mmmm...perhaps not.

New to this, please be gentle! Looking for fun and new friends, maybe more.

Hmm, yeah, that sounded OK. Happy with that I started to look through some of the men that were on offer. I read somewhere that it takes just three seconds when you first see someone for your brain to decide if you're attracted to how they look or not. It's not something we are really conscious about or can control, just a reflex decision our brain makes on our behalf. Sometimes of course attraction can develop later, this is why fat people were usually funny to give them a chance at occasional sex, but for that to happen you have to get to know someone a little first. This was impossible to do on Tinder where it was all about looks and that initial visual attraction.

Considering this I was truly gobsmacked when I was looking through the profiles by some of the bloody awful pictures, and later, after a few disappointing dates, some of the misleading ones too. For example, if they put a pic on there from the 1990's I definitely noticed they had aged 20 years when we met. Likewise, those that had put on more than a few extra pounds since that picture where they were looking tanned and skinny on holiday ten years ago - l noticed that too.

Then there was the too perfect, photoshopped posing. It was such a turn off. It's great that you have a nice body. I fully appreciate a well toned physique and the hard work and dedication that goes into achieving that but honestly boys, those naked gym poses with strategically placed hands or with your junk stuffed in a sock are just material for us ladies to giggle over when we get together for a drink not take you seriously as a potential love interest. A perfect body was not at the top of my wish list when it came to boyfriend material. I think like most women, I am perfectly happy as long as you're decent guy even if you do have a squidgy dad bod. Nicer to cuddle up to anyway in my opinion. No, impressive though they were, the naked six pack fellas didn't really do it for me. I much preferred it when they left something to the imagination. I was much more impressed by a nice smile, personality, wit and humour.

Then there was the other end of the scale. They were after all trying to sell themselves here with nothing but a photo so whilst it was good to have a degree of honesty you would think that they would at least try to present themselves at their best. They were trying to get someone to find them attractive enough to strike up a conversation and hopefully arrange a date with and they probably had a one to two second window of opportunity to do this so why the pictures at such bad angles that they had four chins and I could see right up their ridiculously hairy nostrils. Why the frowning? Were they trying to look mysterious and sexy? Well they didn't, they just looked like moody bad tempered arses.

Photos with their kids were a definite no, no. I mean who in their right mind puts photos of their kids on a dating site? OK so they're a dad, and love their kids, an admirable quality but one that should be a given they shouldn't feel the need to put pictures up of themselves with their little darlings to prove they're good dad. Harsh maybe but in my opinion true. Likewise I didn't really want to see several pictures of his dog no matter how cute. He likes animals that's great I do too but one picture of him with fur face was enough. I didn't want to date his dog.

Pictures with someone who was obviously his ex, just weird. His wedding picture in one case, the bride's face obscured with an emoji - seriously? Group shots of him with his mates, a sociable guy I like that but not much use if he didn't put a solo pic up and I didn't know which one was him. Probably the short, fat, ugly (but most likely funny) one. Landscape photos in the lakes, he was an outdoorsy type of guy that was great, but not so great when he was that small in the photograph I couldn't actually make out his features.

Then there were some who didn't bother putting a picture on at all, what was the point in that? Profiles without pictures were like alcohol free wine, totally pointless. Made me suspect that they were either married or vomit inducingly ugly.

One thing I did learn, very quickly, was that you really have to take the whole internet dating process with an enormous pinch of salt. Was it likely I was going to find my soulmate, the love of my life using a dating app? Who knows, why not? Some people do. Jill knew of quite a few happy couples who had met on dating sites and I was somewhat encouraged by this. But even if I didn't meet Mr Right, I was of the right frame of mind to certainly at least have myself some fun looking.

I also discovered that I had to develop quite a thick skin. The world of online dating was a superficial place full of dickheads heroically hiding behind their keyboards, some downright rude fuckwits. I was unlucky enough to come across a couple of the more idiotic, abusive not rights who frequented these sites and I soon learned not to encourage them, they had no lives and were just spoiling for an argument. I would just block them immediately, forget about them and move on. I never let them occupy any of my precious mind space and never let it get per-sonal. I was called all kinds of names, from fat slut to ugly cunt to man hater (seriously!) by morons who didn't know the first thing about me but thought they had a right to pass judge-ment on me and my character because they had graciously deigned to send me a message. At first I would let these messages hurt my feelings and upset me a little. I would play them over and over in my mind and wonder what I had done to deserve such nasty behaviour but I soon came to the realisation that these messages were not actually about me they were about the person sending them and these idiots just weren't worth getting upset over. I would just delete the messages, block them and dismiss them immediately from my mind. They were not worth another second of my time.

I also made myself some rules. The main rule I stuck to was no sex on a first date. I always made this perfectly clear when agreeing to meet for a date and it served me well on several occasions. Another was to always insist on paying my way and buying my fair share of drinks which kind of complimented the no sex one. You would get the occasional guy who would absolutely insist on paying but then expect payment in kind by way of sexual favours. By explicitly explaining my no sex on a first date rule and then reiterating it at the beginning of the date in no uncertain terms and always offering to pay my share I never then felt obliged to give a guy a blow job in his car in return for a steak dinner. Some actually think that it is perfectly acceptable to treat you in this manner, like you are a prostitute bartering your services in return for a meal and a couple of drinks, and of course there was always the occasional tosser who didn't respect your rules but they never got their way, nor a second date. Luckily I never had to resort to it but I wouldn't have hesitated with a swift knee in the bollocks had they crossed the line too far with inappropriate behaviour.

CHAPTER 11

So, back to Tinder, as I said as far as internet dating goes you really can't get much more straightforward. However on my first effort, being a bit dim sometimes and the type of person that can't be arsed to read instructions properly, I didn't quite grasp it and ended up swiping right on everybody. Liking them all. Every single male on Tinder within a 50 mile radius over the age of 35. There were quite a lot of them.

I later discovered some people actually do this on purpose, liking everyone. I think it's an ego thing to see just how many people are swiping right for you as on Tinder you can only see mutual likes. Others I think are just desperate, casting their nets far and wide hoping for any catch at all. In my case though it was a genuine error. I thought if you liked someone you had to click on the heart symbol which is an alternative to swiping right, very confusing in my opinion. Please just give me one option so I can't go wrong. Needless to say I was then inundated with messages from undesirables that I had inadvertently liked and had no clue how to unlike

Jill turned up later that afternoon to find me puzzling over all the messages I was receiving.

"I thought they could only message you if you matched and I thought you could only match if both liked each other?" I said gesturing at my full inbox.

"Yep" she confirmed "That's how it works."

"Well I haven't even liked anyone yet but I've got all these matches and messages!"

"What have you been doing?" She asked looking through the messages "Bloody hell, pervert Stan age 67 wants to have bareback menstrual sex with you, what the fuck?! Kinky old bastard."

There were quite a few messages along these lines, one or two even offering payment in return for sexual services. I was offended, did I look like a bloody prostitute?

"It's because you used the word "fun" in your profile" explained Jill as I vented my outrage and offence "that translates to sex in some Neanderthal man brains. The male population of Tinder that are perverts, which is the majority of them, think you are offering your services."

Bloody hell.

After looking through and marvelling at some of the messages and profiles we decided it would be easiest just to delete the account and start over again. So, with a new profile set up, this time without using the word "fun" in the bio I finally got a couple of matches that I did actually like the look of and sent some messages. Some even replied back. Why do some like you and then when you match and you say hello ignore or immediately delete you? Just rude. Anyway, before I knew it I'd arranged my very first internet date. It was, in no uncertain terms, a complete and utter disaster.

He had seemed so promising but I soon came to realise that you simply cannot judge someone correctly until you meet in the real world. An online persona can be a million miles away from a real life one and people rarely look like their profile pictures. It's like when you order that dress from China that you've seen online for the bargain price of a tenner. It's a beautiful cocktail dress suitable for a film star to wear at a premiere in the pictures but when it eventually arrives - six weeks later because you are too tight to pay for express shipping, it is shapeless, badly sewn, totally different in colour to what you were expecting and the wrong size. The material is thin and cheap, probably made from recycled carrier bags and you would be too nervous to stand within ten feet of a naked flame whilst wearing it. Obviously you should know better, if it seems too good to be true and all that but we keep ordering the shit from China anyway in the hope that one day it will be just like the picture and it will fit.

That's a bit like online dating. Keep on clicking, keep on hoping, keep on being disappointed.

So I got my first proper, non-accidental, match

on Tinder, Justin. Justin and I chatted by message for a while then progressed to telephone conversations. We got on really well, appeared to have lots in common having a bit of a laugh on the phone and several long and interesting chats. Could he be potential boyfriend material? Could it really be that easy? We arranged a date agreeing to meet up at a pub for a bite to eat.

The big day arrived. I was very, very nervous, it had been a good eleven years or so since I had been on an actual date after all. I almost called it off several times but instead bought a new outfit that I couldn't really afford and spent a significant amount of time, i.e. more than five minutes on my hair and makeup. There wasn't much I could do to hide the chubby tummy, it was beyond the aid of mere control pants. I wasted thirteen quid on some shorts made out of some shiny, black, extra strong, elasticated material that claimed to be able to give me a flat tummy. But no, they didn't hold it in as promised, just changed it from unformed and squishy to rounded and hard. They took me about ten minutes of huffing and puffing to get on and made me look quite pregnant instead of merely a bit fat. On the plus side the new outfit was quite flattering, my hair was behaving itself for once and I was quite pleased with what I saw in the mirror. Happy with the end result and thinking I looked reasonably attractive or at the very least fairly presentable off I went.

I arrived at the pub and spotted Justin waiting for me near the door. Taking a deep breath, trying to keep my nerves under control and counselling myself that it would be fine, I walked over to him. I could feel his eyes scrutinising me as I walked across making me feel very uncomfortable but then he smiled at me and I began to feel a little better. Unfortunately though that feeling didn't last very long when his first words to me, in a nice, loud, booming voice so the whole world could hear, were "Well you're a bit fatter than I was expecting - har! har!"

Although said in a jovial manner this greeting didn't exactly get us off to the best of starts and definitely didn't do much for my already low self esteem or my first date jitters. Yes, admittedly I was overweight but I had never attempted to hide this fact. My profile pictures were clear and current and included a full length one. I had also included in my description that I was a curvy girl. We all know this is a polite way of saying hey look I'm a chubster, a BBW so if you're looking for slim then just swipe left - thank you! And anyway, Justin was shorter, a lot older and a lot fatter than he looked in his pictures. I thought of replying "Well mate you're fat, ugly, bald and fucking rude!" but I managed to bite my tongue. Just.

He had described himself as 5ft 11 when he was actually shorter than me, I was wearing flat shoes and I'm only 5ft 4. His build, he said, was athletic, hmmmm OK, a long retired athlete who was now rather fond of fast food maybe. He had also said he had dark hair, but was wearing hats in all of his profile pictures. Maybe he'd had dark hair a decade or so ago but certainly not anymore, his head was as bald and shiny as a cue ball. Not that I have any issue with bald, there are some very sexy bald men (although not in this case) I am just not very impressed with people who try to make out they're something they're not.

What followed was one of the slowest and most excruciating hours of my life. I wish I'd had the guts to say from the off, well clearly there's no chemistry here, nice to meet you but we may as well not bother dickhead! I definitely would now rather than wasting my time, but I still had an awful lot to learn about this dating lark, and I was just too polite for my own good.

Justin's main topic of conversation, apart from self-professing how wonderful and successful he was and telling me in great detail about all the expensive, designer things he owned, was how this gorgeous, young, blonde, slim - emphasis on slim - girl fancied him like mad but how he wouldn't go there because she was a single mum with young children. Although he'd happily bang her in a heartbeat who could be bothered with all that baggage? Nice guy. Just what you want to chat about on a first date and if young, blonde and slim was what floated his boat then why arrange a date with a fat, older brunette?

The obnoxious idiot wittered on and on, spitting food everywhere and I began to entertain fantasies of stabbing him to death with my fork. I had to make my excuses and leave before I did something I would probably be arrested for. Needless to say we didn't meet again but at least he was polite enough to insist on paying for the meal, which I was very self-conscious about eating under the circumstances. I ordered a salad and only managed to choke half of it down even though I was ravenous and I really wanted a big fat plate of fish and chips!

So unsurprisingly that didn't develop into romance but rather than letting this unpleasant encounter put me off or get me down I chalked it up to experience and got straight back to it. Checking my messages I got chatting to Dave and made arrangements to meet him a couple of days later.

Happily my first date with Dave was much, much better. Didn't bother with all the phone calls and stuff beforehand just suggested we meet straight away for a drink. I had already learned my first lesson, there was no point in wasting time getting to know someone I might hate in real life. We met up for a drink (no food this time another lesson learned) got on well with each other and had a good laugh. He didn't seem to mind that I was a bit of a fatty or if he did he at least had the good manners to keep his opinion to himself. It was a pleasant evening, nothing too outstanding but it was nice enough and nice is all you need sometimes. We met about a week later for a second date, it went well and so when he invited me back to his place I thought why not?

For some reason, rebound, revenge or maybe the fact that I just like sex, I'd felt this mad urgency to sleep with someone after my breakup. Anyone really, I wasn't particularly fussy. I think I just needed to get something out of my system. Apart from the disastrous one night stand where I had been so drunk I couldn't even remember if I had sex, never mind if it was any good, I hadn't slept with anyone for months and anyone but my ex for far too many years. So even though I wasn't overly attracted to Dave, was totally embarrassed about the state of my body and I had no decent, flattering underwear that fitted me I wanted to have sex with him. He was available, willing, able (I hoped), clean, not repulsive or noticeably weird, appeared to like me so he'd do.

We went back to his place, it was a bit of a dump to be honest, a good clean wouldn't have gone amiss. His toilet seat was broken, he had no hand soap and only one threadbare towel that I could see in the bathroom but he did have the single male requisite 96" HD TV and PlayStation 17 (or whichever number we were up to) and the black leather recliner sofa. We had a quick coffee then up to bed we went.

Truthfully the sex wasn't great. Actually it was disappointingly rather shit. It lasted about 37 seconds, no foreplay at all, none, not even a quick, cursory tweak of a nipple. Without the benefit of alcohol induced confidence I was very self-conscious when I got undressed, worrying about what Dave would think when he saw the state of my body and the way it was oozing out of my not very sexy, overwashed, too-small under garments. I insisted the light went out, stripped in matter of seconds and immediately dove under the covers, but in all honesty I don't think he even noticed my body. Or if he did, he didn't care. I think he was just happy with the thought of getting his end away.

He got in bed beside me, climbed aboard and away he went. He gave a couple of thrusts, made a funny face, a little groan and it was all over. I'm guessing it had been a while for him too. All that worrying about my body for something that lasted less than a minute.

Despite the disappointing sex it was still nice to be held and have that physical contact, even if only for a little while, and to know that some-one didn't find my body as utterly repulsive as I thought it was at that time. I didn't stay the night but that was my choice. He didn't ask me or even hint for me to leave after the main event but I couldn't cope with the post-coital awkwardness never mind face the awkwardness of waking up with him the next morning. We lay side by side afterwards. Strangely, despite having just been intimate we were being very careful not to touch each other and stared at the ceiling chatting politely for around ten minutes about really random stuff such as wallpaper paste and bamboo socks. When I thought a respectable amount of time had passed, even though I couldn't see a clock, wasn't wearing a watch and couldn't see my phone I said "Wow! Would you look at the time, I really must get going."

That was our one and only night of, erm well don't know what to call it really it wasn't exactly passion. Anyway we didn't bother repeating it. We did have a third date, not sure why probably just out of politeness but it was just really awkward. I acknowledged and accepted that there was no chemistry between us, I didn't even really like him all that much and he was wearing the most awful shoes. It's one of my weird foibles, no matter how attractive the man horrible shoes just turn me right off, I can't help it. We exchanged a few short *"How are you?" "I'm good thanks, how are you?"* type text messages over the next few days, again probably just out of politeness but we didn't see each other again and eventually just lost contact. I wasn't devastated or even the least bit sad. No big loss. He certainly was never going to be the love of my life and he was pretty shit in bed.

CHAPTER 12

The depressing, lonely, first singleton Christmas came and went, grey, dark and wet to match my mood. Then my birthday. I hate having a January birthday. People with January birthdays are ripped off when it comes to presents. There is absolutely no point in having an Amazon wish list if you're a January baby because January babies just get re-gifted their friend's unwanted Christmas presents, especially if, like mine, your birthday is before payday and everyone is still skint from the festive season. No one can afford to go out with you to celebrate either so you usually end up alone and depressed with a cheap bottle of wine and six Bayliss and Harding gift sets that you will end up taking to the charity shop in March, donating to the church spring fayre tombola stall or re-re-gifting to your great auntie or gran.

I had chatted online to a couple more guys but didn't get around to arranging any more dates for a while. Even after only two dates I was already feeling a little down and jaded with the whole online dating thing. I was also disgusted by the state of my body. Looking at myself in the mirror I decided I wouldn't even consider having sex with anyone else until I had lost some weight and gained some confidence and so concentrated on that for a while. I forced myself to go on a diet, overcame the frappe addiction by repeating the mantra "three hundred and fifty calories, three hundred and fifty calories" whenever I was in the vicinity of a McDonalds and pleasingly the weight started to come off. Once I stopped with the crap convenience foods and takeaways and cut down on the booze I lost quite a bit fairly quickly going down a couple of dress sizes which in turn boosted my confidence no end. After a couple of months I decided it was time to get back out there and I finally arranged another date.

Greg was very, very short and so small in build he could have shopped for clothes in the children's section. I felt like a giant next to him and I'm only little really. I'm not certain how tall he said he was on his profile but I'm quite sure it wasn't the truth. Now, although admittedly I do prefer the taller, chunkier model, I don't have an issue with smaller guys but as I have previously said I do have an issue with fanciful descriptions. Also, to be honest the idea of having to bend down to kiss my man doesn't really do it for me. So it didn't really get off to the best of starts when I was expecting to meet someone who I'm sure said in his profile was taller or at least the same height as me and it turned out he probably only just scraping five foot.

That aside Greg turned out to be lovely, great company and we had a very pleasant afternoon but there was definitely no chemistry there, at least not for me. Because I had enjoyed his company we went on a second date, however I made it - or at least I thought I had made it perfectly clear that he was firmly friend-zoned. I did actually say it straight to him that I was not interested in anything other than friendship, there was just no chemistry there for me. He was going through a rather messy divorce and I was under the impression that he was OK with that, happy just to have a female friend to talk to.

A week or so later we went to an open mic night at a local bar. He had told me he sang a little and played guitar and he was going to play that night. I wasn't busy so I thought I would go along to support him. Oh dear. When he serenaded me with his shaky version of Queens' "Save Me" actually getting down on one knee and pointedly singing the line "to start again with someone new" whilst gazing longingly into my eyes it became clear that he hadn't quite grasped the friend-zone thing after all.

He messaged me a few days later telling me he would love to take me to this place in France where you could camp in a clear perspex tent shaped like a bubble, so our first night together could be under the stars, very special and romantic. Now, whilst thoroughly intrigued with this bubble camping concept, (what about privacy?) I was never, ever going to have sex with this man-boy and had to spell it out to him very clearly at that point that I just wasn't into him in that way. In fact I thought it best not to see him again at all so I definitely wouldn't continue to give him the wrong impression or any false hope. Whilst there was nothing wrong with him, apart from being a bit on the small side, he was just not for me and I genuinely hope he found himself a lovely lady to serenade with Queen and have sex in a bubble tent with.

Jumping from one extreme to the next, Martin came in at a giraffe like 6ft 11. He was ridiculously tall in comparison to me and very, very slim which made him appear even taller. He also turned up on our date wearing the ugliest man shoes I had ever seen in my whole life. Like a cheap, man made, black leather effect plastic canal barge with huge velcro fasteners!! WTF?! Whereas I can totally sympathise with the fact that he had limited footwear options with his enormous size 15 feet surely he could have found something a little less like a giant's version of a shoe a five year old from a destitute family would wear especially in these wonderful modern days of internet shopping.

Martin was actually a nice enough chap and reasonably attractive despite the freakish height but my strange brain could not get past those awful shoes. Besides, with him being almost two foot taller than me, dating him would have been logistically problematic. He was also the worst kisser ever. The goodbye kiss, I go for the thanks but no thanks, see ya later quick dry peck on the cheek, he goes for full on tonsil tennis. Huge, wet, slobbery, probing fat tongue and big sucky lips. Urgh.

Next!

Next came Paul. He looked rather cute on his profile pictures and was very funny to talk to on the phone. I do like a man who can make me laugh. It was a warm evening and we met at a little pub with a beer garden. Getting a couple of drinks and sitting outside I noticed he was shaking a little and put it down to nerves. However when he then fell over his own feet a couple of times and then a curb I realised he was actually rather pissed. Concerned I asked him if he had driven. He told me he had got the bus so he could have "a couple of tinnies" on the way to settle his nerves. He then admitted he had lost his driving licence for drink driving and was due to get it back in a couple of months. He assured me he wasn't an alcoholic but given he necked three drinks to my one and then went on to tell me how he was no longer allowed to see his kids due to his drinking and that he had recently been sacked for being pissed on the job I was beginning to think that maybe he was kidding himself.

Making my excuses I left wishing him luck but saying we wouldn't be meeting again. He was genuinely perplexed by this. He was under the impression we had got on great and was already planning a romantic weekend in the lake district together for our next date. No doubt with a cool box full of alcoholic beverages. Sure that sounded great, but not for me, not in this lifetime.

I nipped into a nearby supermarket on my way home and as I was paying for my shopping he came staggering in, probably to purchase a couple more beers for the bus journey home. I hurriedly tried to hide behind my bag for life but he spotted me, and waved.

"Hey, forgot to tell you - nice tits!" he shouted. Great, I thought as everyone looked first at him then at my boobs.

He then came over to me and tried his best to convince me to go back to his house with him for a couple of drinks, it'd be a right laugh he assured me. Yeah I'm sure.

"Thanks but no thanks, I think I'll pass." I told him.

Just when I thought I'd heard the last of him, about an hour later he phoned to tell me he'd missed his last bus home and asked would I go pick him up from the bus station and give him a lift? Er, that would be a no, goodbye - block!

Not one to be put off easily I quickly arranged

another date but I didn't even make it out of my car this time.

I was sat in my car ready to get out and meet farmer John at the pre-arranged spot when I saw him come lurching down the street. He was absolutely filthy, dressed in dirty, ripped clothes and really did lurch as though one leg was several inches shorter than the other. I hid my face and luckily, even though I'd given him a clear description of my car's make, model and colour, he just continued to lurch on straight past me. He then went to stand on the opposite side of the road studying the oncoming traffic with great intensity. No doubt searching for my car which was parked in full view not twenty feet away from him. Maybe a higher power had turned me and my car invisible to save me from this strange man?

I sat in my car and watched him for a moment, undecided about what to do. My natural politeness at odds with the desire to just get the hell out of there, fast. In the end I just thought sod it, and drove back home again. Sorry but there was no way I was being seen in public with that man.

I was then inundated with texts that just got stranger and stranger along the lines of..

```
Please baby, me and you that's what
it's all about it is this thing is
please xx
```

and a puzzling

```
Baby stop spinning stings come on I'm
here, I'll wait for you forever circle
back circle back xx
```

What does that even mean? I'd had about thirty texts from him in the twenty minutes it took me to drive home. I messaged back to apologise for being a bit rude and standing him up but saying sorry he just wasn't for me and then blocked him.
  My natural optimism was starting to wane a little at this point but I plodded on and arranged another date. Sadly yet another disaster.

It was a gorgeous spring day so I had arranged to meet Gary one Sunday afternoon for a walk at a local park. I pulled up and spotted him waiting for me at the side of the road. I couldn't help but stare. He was really tall and broad with an extraordinarily small head in comparison to the rest of him. His tiny head was completely bald, shiny and curiously pointed on top just like an egg. His ears were huge, sticking out almost at right angles to his strange head like one of those baby sippy cups with two handles.
  Spotting me he grinned my way flashing the biggest teeth I had ever seen on a human being. They were like tombstones and very, very white. He certainly wasn't a handsome man. His profile pic-

ture, which I recall was a little blurry, must have been taken at a very flattering angle to minimise these alarming features.

He worked at a local supermarket but he should have been an actor. He would have made a fortune in horror flicks looking right at home chomping on someone's leg with those gnashers. I found him quite scary to be honest and I'm glad the park was busy with plenty of people milling around.

I became aware that I was staring in rude, slack jawed wonderment at this extraordinary ugly man, that my engine was still running and that I had coasted perilously close to another car. I think I was in mild shock. I forced myself to blink, put on my handbrake and turned off my engine before I caused an accident. Fixing a smile to my face I got out of my car and I walked over to him already formulating my escape plan in my mind.

I know looks aren't everything and I wish I could say he redeemed himself with his wonderful personality but nah, nope, afraid not. His opening line was "Hey! Glad you agreed to meet at the park, I hate wasting money buying a woman a drink when I might not get a shag out of it" his closing line, delivered with a terrifying grin and even more terrifying wink " Give me a call if you're interested in taking this further, I'm really good in bed. Don't be waiting for me to call you because I never do the chasing."

What a shame it was then that I somehow managed to lose his number. I missed out on a real charmer there. He had told me he had a son. I really cannot get over the fact that someone, willingly I'm hoping, had sex with this man and produced a child. I can only hope the poor boy took after his mother.

CHAPTER 13

It was time to up my game and get serious in my search for Mr Right, or at least Mr Right Now. Up until now the only men I seemed to be attracting were the Mr Not Rights and I was beginning to worry I'd never again have sex, or at least decent sex with anything that didn't require batteries. I needed to be more upfront and honest about what I was looking for and a lot more choosy with who I agreed to meet. I joined a couple more dating sites, those that required a little more in depth information than Tinder and looked through the profiles with increasing despair. All I was looking for was a straight man, preferably sane and reasonably presentable who was fairly good in bed and with whom I had a mutual attraction. Apparently such a thing was as rare as unicorn shit.

Jill laughed as I told her about my recent dates "Don't bother buying a lotto ticket" she chuckled "You obviously cannot pick a winner. Right, come on mate, strip off it's make over time. If you're not the best version of you then you've no hope of finding a decent man."

Jill's makeovers were legendary, she had a great eye for style and her no nonsense approach to everything was brutal but very effective. You could trust her to tell you the truth about everything even though it sometimes hurt your feelings and made you want to cry.

My obligatory post-breakup makeover was a good six months overdue so I stripped to my underwear and we critically appraised my body in the mirror, starting with my hair. Although psychotherapy and anger management is probably what most of us really need when we go through a breakup, a lot of women just go get a new haircut and/or colour. Tempted though I was to go for a radical change there wasn't really much to be done about my hair. Longish and dark, as I had worn it for pretty much most of my life, it was OK the way it was. I suffer from perpetual Bad Hair Day. No amount of coaxing, expensive products or clever cuts ever make any difference to my stubborn, scruffy, lank locks so I have given up trying and just leave it now to grow any damn wild way it pleases. Lobbing off split ends occasionally and chucking a home colour on every now and again to hide the stubborn strands of tinsel that appear is about as much attention as it deserves.

Whenever I had gotten bored of my bonce and tried to deviate from this style or colour it was always with disastrous consequences. I did once, for some strange reason, decide to have my hair all chopped off and bleached blonde. It wasn't a great look to be honest. Especially when you have a big fat moon face as I did at the time. I was hoping for a cute little pixie look but the actual look I got I could have had a starring role in Orange is The New Black as the stereotypical big butch lesbian. I think I was also under the impression that this would be a low maintenance do but that was not the case. Every single morning you could guarantee it would be stuck out at right angles at one side and completely flat on the other. A good amount of time was begrudgingly wasted and various disgustingly sticky, expensive products employed to try to convince the stubborn yellow tufts to lay the right way. I'm not good in the morning as it is and can't be arsed faffing with my hair at the best of times so I was suitably unimpressed by this. Typically this was the hairstyle I had when I needed to renew my passport and driving licence. I cringe with embarrassment every time I have to show them to someone. Should have worn a wig. Never mind, only five more years to go until I can get new ones...

So, reasonably happy with my hair or at least, having learned my lesson from past mistakes we accepted that was as good as it got. We continued with a critical evaluation of my body focusing on the positives but acknowledging the negatives. By this time I had lost a good few pounds and was feeling a whole lot better about myself. Sure,

I'd never be a supermodel, or have a flat stomach and my boobs would never again be what could be described as pert, at least not without surgical intervention, but what I was seeing was no longer utterly repulsive and I was fairly proud of myself for shifting most of the flab. As it had been quite sunny, I'd managed to get a bit of a tan and my skin was lovely and soft from my lifelong addiction with expensive body butter.

Although my boobs were no longer perky, especially after the weight loss, they were still generous and in fairly reasonable shape. Yes they were a little droopy and tended to go try to hide under my armpits when I was lay on my back but at least my nipples were still pointed mostly forwards rather than at the floor.

I am a bit of a short arse and have chunky short limbs, not much I can do about that but at least my arms and legs were no longer morbidly obese, unshapely appendages. I was thrilled to note I actually had a bit of a thigh gap going on once more. Whilst I still had bingo wings they were getting much smaller and I didn't feel overly conscious about wearing sleeveless tops any more. With the aid of a good fitting bra and knickers I considered that I actually looked pretty decent in clothes and thought I would no longer die of shame if someone saw me naked. Other areas though had been a little neglected and were in dire need of some urgent attention. I'm lucky not to have much in the way of body hair. Much to the envy of my friends I never even have to shave my legs. My lady bush though, now that was a different story. It was completely out of control. Totally neglected. It looked as if a very small Rastafarian was peeping through my thighs.

Let us take a brief interlude here to talk about intimate grooming. Ladies, your garden should be clean, fresh, nicely trimmed and welcoming at all times. Or not. It's entirely up to you, it is after all your body. If you want a hairy paradise then go for it. Your muff, minge, pussy, mucky, wizards sleeve, growler, silk purse, furry axe wound, fanny, the ever lovely twat or cunt and my personal all time biggest turnoff - love tunnel, whatever you want to call it and whoever you invite to frolic in it is entirely your business and bugger all to do with anyone else.

Ah, love tunnel. That brings back some fond memories of sex with someone I once had a short relationship with. The lovely Richard. Every single time we were getting down to it Richard would say, in all seriousness and with great enthusiasm, "Baby, I'm gonna put my big train into your love tunnel"

I was always dying to reply "All aboard, choo! choo!" but I think it may have ruined the moment, especially given my predisposition for bursting into hysterical laughter at the most inappropriate times. I just had to pretend not to hear him and ignore the train whistle sounding off in my imagination.

He was a genuinely nice guy, great cook too. Yes, that's not a misspelling, cook not cock, his Sunday roasts were to die for and food is up there in my top three favourite reasons for being alive. He did however have rather an off-putting fetish. He liked to conclude our sex sessions, which by the way (apart from the train reference) were otherwise very satisfactory, by ejaculating all over my back, boobs or belly. Then enthusiastically licking it off.

Yummy.

Unfortunately this fondness for savouring his own spunk was a little too much for me, turned my stomach somewhat, so that particular romance didn't last very long. Shame really could have had a good thing there.

Back to the forbidden forest. To shave or not to shave? If you are proud of your panty whiskers and thigh brows or you simply cannot be arsed with the upkeep then don't ever feel pressured into complying to please a man, although my personal research has concluded that the vast majority of men do prefer a closely trimmed or even fully shaved beaver. Bare or not, it should go without saying, personal cleanliness is at the top of most people's wish list especially in your intimate areas. Sweaty crotches, dirty dicks and fishy fannies have got to be a big no no. Saying that, although I've yet to speak to a woman who digs a cheesy cock, some men do like a big hairy smelly muff, but then some men also like to be pissed or shat on, each to their own.

On the subject of toilet play I've been reliably informed that some men have uses for glass pan lids that are nothing to do with cooking. They lie back and cover their face with the glass lid holding them by putting the knobs in their mouths, (the knobs on the lids that is, not their own knobs). The rest I'll leave to your imagination but suffice to say it allows an extremely up close and personal view of something that I certainly wouldn't want to be seeing, without it getting in your eyes. Whatever turns you on I suppose but personally just the thought of toilet play makes me want to vomit up my dinner.

On with intimate grooming. If you like your man to give you an Australian kiss then he'd probably prefer not to have your short and curlies stuck between his teeth. Perhaps the only thing worse after oral sex than flossing with pubes is finding shit on your chin. But getting rid of the excess shrubbery can be problematic. Unlike the precious hair on my head that simply falls out without any encouragement at all happily blocking up drains and garnishing food everywhere I go, my pussy whiskers are remarkably resilient, stubborn little bastards, firmly anchored in there like limpets on a rock.

Shaving is the most obvious, cheapest, easiest

and least painful way to go but you never get that lovely smooth finish that you are promised with the ads. You go buy the pretty little sparkly purple or pink lady razor suitable for intimate areas, which is probably just a cheaper man razor in drag. Parting with a not inconsiderable amount of your hard earned cash in exchange for the promise of the smooth, silky skin of a love goddess. Expensive they may be but please don't even consider buying the cheap razors, may as well just hack off your pubes with a bread knife you'll get the same result.

Soap up and shave, it can be a little tricky to get into all the nooks and crannies if you're going for a Hollywood and you may have to get into some strange positions to access all areas but afterwards you are indeed a smooth, silky goddess. Well at least for a short while before your vagina turns into a cactus.

After about an hour there are a million tiny and amazingly sharp prickles poking through your knickers making them feel like they are made from Velcro. And that post shave itch, Jesus. The day after you shave the itch will be driving you demented. You obviously cannot walk around scratching at your groin in public, although it may make people respect your personal space and give you a bit more room on a crowded train if you did so.

What about other, more lasting ways to get rid of the pesky pubes? Hair removal cream simply does not work in that area, well at least it didn't for me with my resilient super-pubes and unless you are a serious masochist other methods are not really to be advised. Intimate waxing anyone? Much less painful to set your darn gorilla mask on fire and douse the flames with vinegar. I tried this once, waxing my intimate area not setting it on fire that is. I did it at home with wax strips designed for "sensitive" areas. It was definitely not one of the best ideas I've ever had. Following the instructions I heated up and applied two strips - one on each side thinking I would work my way inward evenly, my ever optimistic mind imagining a lovely neat landing strip surrounded by smooth silky skin. Taking a deep breath I took hold of the first strip and ripped it off with a good, fast tug. I cried. It took me forty five minutes, three shots of vodka and a soak in a hot bath to loosen the wax before I was brave enough to remove the second strip.

I did half consider going to the beauticians, and letting the professionals do the job. However the thought of a perfectly made up sadistic nineteen year old inflicting pain whilst staring at my sad old muff was just too much to bear. I'd want to shout "yours will look like this too once you've had a couple of kids and a few good bashings you smug young lady!" When I had my eyebrows done they commented on the "lovely shape" of my brow. I dread to think of the conversation whilst they massacred my pokey... " that's a nice plump one, lovely voluptuous vulva, nice even lip size. Shame about the stretch marks, we have some cream for that."

Yes, the removal of the pubes revealed I have stretch marks down below and yes I would probably part with sixty quid for the miracle fanny stretch mark cream out of pure shame.

So I shaved, plucked, exfoliated and moisturised. Hacked off my split ends, dyed my greys and went shopping with Jill to buy some sexy but impractical new underwear that I could hide in the bathroom or my handbag to sneakily change into from my firm support granny pants if sex was on the cards. I was ready to bare all and get down to some serious action.

One problem, I still needed a man to help me out with this. With renewed optimism back on Tinder I went and arranged a date with Ian who sounded terribly posh. The day of the date I decided I needed a bit of a pamper and booked myself in at the local beauticians for a nice Swedish hot stone massage. After the lovely massage, feeling all chilled and relaxed Sally the head honcho in charge at Diamonds Beauty informed me that they had a special offer on eyebrow tint and wax and asked me if I would be interested. Why not I thought, my eyebrows were a bit sparse and it would save me having to pencil them in every morning. Also Sally was a bit scary and hard to say no to so I told her to go for it.

"Great" she said and went to work, cheerfully announcing "All done" 15 minutes later and shoving a mirror in my face.

I considered my reflection in shocked silence. Where my eyebrows used to sit quietly and unobtrusively I was now the proud owner of two very black, very bushy caterpillars that screamed "HEY! LOOK AT ME!!!!!" from my pale face.

"Oh" I managed to say "They're a little darker than I was expecting"

"They'll fade a little" she assured me

"When?" I asked, thinking of the date I had lined up that evening.

"A day or two" she said "They'll need redoing in three to four weeks"

Shit.

That night I took my new eyebrows to meet my date, Posh Ian. It was pissing it down and typically I couldn't find my umbrella. I had to go on the date wearing the only waterproof coat I owned, an old flasher mac with the hood up looking like a sad librarian trainspotting spinster. Predictably the date was a total disaster anyway. He had sold himself as a gentleman on-line and was awfully posh but also awfully rude trying to cop a feel of my tits in the car park when I went to give him a quick kiss goodbye forever. Some sodding gentleman.

Block.

CHAPTER 14

I was getting a little bored with Tinder there were no new potential victims on there it was all the same old faces so I decided to branch out a little and sign up to Plenty of Fish. I'd heard lots of horror stories about this site, been warned it was basically a hook up site but frankly who cared? It's not as if I was looking for love or even a serious relationship at that point. A friends with benefits relationship, or fuck buddy if you want to be crude would be about just right. I'd also been told that I would get loads of dick pics and indecent proposals on this site, well I'm a big girl I can handle that. Although why men feel the urge to send dick pics is beyond me. "Hi, I'm Jason. I'd love to take you out sometime. Here's an unsolicited picture of my unimpressive, not very photogenic, four whole inches of man meat to try to convince you to come on a date with me. If that doesn't work I may send you a cum shot, or even better, a wank video."

Boys, this behaviour is a little off putting if I'm going to be totally honest. Could you imagine if women did that? "Pleased to meet you, here's a picture of my growler, fancy a date?" mind you, most of the perverts that peruse the dating sites would probably love it if you did.

I was in the firm, familiar grip of insomnia once again and it was 4am when I uploaded my photo and wrote my profile. I just put an ordinary snapshot of myself on there, nothing sexy just me in jeans and T-shirt, hardly any makeup, my everyday look. Didn't want to encourage the perves, not that they actually need much in the way of encouragement. I finished my new profile, shut down my laptop, managed to shake the insomnia loose and grabbed a few hours sleep.

I woke up around 8.30am, made coffee and fired up my laptop. Curious but not expecting much yet I signed back into POF. It works a little differently to Tinder in that you can just message anyone straight off you don't have to match first and I was amazed to find that I had over fifty messages already. In just four hours and the early hours of the morning at that. Wow, OK then. I was not the only sad insomniac cruising the dating apps and there was an obvious female deficit on there. I was also a new fish so getting lots of attention from all the thirsty guys and of course there is also the fact that I am devastatingly attractive, haha! Seriously, although pleasing to the ego lots of messages may be, let's take a reality check here. Most of these guys were just looking for their leg over and would probably shag anything with a pulse.

The messages were from a weird and wonderful variety of men and even one or two women even though I had clearly stated I was heterosexual in my profile. Big and small, all ethnicities, wildly varied ages. I even had one from an emaciated, bald old man who was dressed in a wedding gown and wearing immaculate full makeup including bright red lipstick.

I scrolled through immediately discounting the majority of the messages. Normally I'm polite and would try to at least acknowledge someone who has taken the time to contact me but as these messages were unsolicited and most were probably copied and pasted with quite a few along the lines of "gorgeous eyes, how would you like to sit on my face?" I didn't worry myself too much with dating etiquette.

One or two messages did interest me. I peeked at the profiles and responded to a couple. One in particular intrigued me, it was from a guy called Ste who had a profile picture of a young Steve McQueen. I love the Hollywood actors from the 60's and 70's, one of my all time favourite films is one Steve McQueen starred in, The Towering Inferno. Watching old, badly acted, corny crap disaster movies whilst snuggled under a blanket and eating my bodyweight in junk food is one of my most enjoyable rainy Sunday afternoon pastimes.

I took a peek at Ste's profile. It was total cheese, along the lines of:-

Still searching for my beautiful soulmate. Looking to spend cosy nights in beside my open fire drinking wine and sharing kisses and cuddles

Like I said, pure Cheddar and probably total bollocks, he was most likely just looking for a shag. His message was complementary and to the point if not overly original and I decided to message him back;

>*Hey, you have nice eyes and a beauti ful smile. Fancy a chat?*

Thanks! Sure. Tell me a bit about yourself

Why the Steve McQueen profile pic?

Just wary of my privacy, I've no problem sending you a picture of the real me via private message x

I'm not sure why I decided to message him, I wouldn't normally message someone who didn't have a genuine profile picture but despite this and the corniness of his profile I did. He was online, so we got chatting immediately. He sent me a picture of his real self and I realised it was someone I had actually known for quite some time. I had worked with him several years ago and we were Facebook friends. Small world. He remembered me too and invited me to go visit him for a brew and a catch-up. From what I remembered he'd been pretty good looking, although a bit full of himself but we'd always got on well and had a bit of a laugh. From the picture he sent to me he still looked a bit of alright and we were getting along great on the chat so I thought why not, what did I have to lose?

I drove over to his house later that afternoon and we got reacquainted, a lot more intimately than we had previously. He was still good looking, he smelt fantastic, was well dressed and, bonus points, was wearing great shoes. We caught up having a great afternoon gossiping about the various people we both knew and laughing a lot over coffee and chocolate biscuits. After a short while I realised I was starting to feel a little turned on and excited, there was definitely sexual chemistry there. Lots of eye contact, flirtatious behaviour and innuendo was going on. Sex was definitely on the cards and I was so ready and willing to break my first date no sex rule. I didn't think it needed to apply as we already knew each other. In any case I was horny, in the middle of a sex famine and eager to take advantage of the situation. It didn't seem like he had any objections to first date sex either (I think most men don't) and after finishing our second coffee he took my cup and moved in for a snog.

It turned out he was a fantastic kisser. Slow, sensual just the right amount of tongue action. He also nibbled at and kissed my neck which I find a massive turn on. We had a good fifteen minutes of that, I was tingling with desire and was oh so ready for some sex which I was fervently hoping would be on the cards very soon. Just as I was about to pounce on him and rip his clothes off he finally suggested we take it up to the bedroom. I eagerly agreed silently praying "Please be good in bed, please be good in bed" as I followed him quickly up the stairs.

Once in his bedroom my clothes were removed with great speed and no regard or appreciation for the sexy new flattering underwear that I just happened to be wearing on the off chance that such an encounter may occur. It had cost me a small fortune and taken me ages to choose but to my disgust it was just ripped off without a second look and discarded to the floor, an expensive little pile of black lace.

Carrying on with the delicious kissing and neck nibbling he pushed me back onto the bed. He then caressed my breasts, gently biting and licking my nipples. I was squirming with desire. His erection was pushing invitingly against my thigh increasing my lust and making me quiver with anticipation. I was very happy with the discovery that his dick was quite big, I silently thanked the heavens and prayed that he knew what to do with it.

It was all looking good so far.

He turned his attention from my breasts to focus on what was between my legs. His hand at first gently touching, exploring and teasing. Oh yes! Sadly it all then went seriously to shit when his fingers went after my clitoris, rubbing at it with the fevered enthusiasm of a gambling addict going at a pile of scratch cards with a two pence piece.

I tried to stop him after a couple of minutes as I feared the friction was about to make my vagina burst into flames but despite my protests he was insistent on carrying on. As he was not showing any signs of slowing down I decided I needed to urgently fake an orgasm. I gave an Oscar winning performance, lots of writhing around and porn star worthy "oohs" and "oooooos" and "ahahahAH's!" but he still didn't stop.

I tried my hardest to push his hand away but he was strong and showed no sign of letting up. I asked him to stop, he just winked at me and told me lie back and enjoy it. How the fuck was I supposed to do that when I had a smouldering bush and was developing blisters on the most sensitive part of my body? By this point I was actually begging him to stop. Nope. He was unrelenting. It was torture. I have no idea what the hell he was trying to prove. Then, in a flash of genius I suggestively whispered to him that I was dying to suck his cock. That worked. Finally! My poor abused clit escaped the clutches of his evil, overzealous fingers.

Can't say the oral experience was much better. I pride myself on giving good head, have been complimented on my technique a few times, but his idea of being sucked off was to basically fuck my mouth. He grabbed my hair forcing my head up and down almost making me gag. I'm sure I'm not the only woman who hates it when a man does that. I like to be in control when there's a dick in my mouth.

Enough was enough and I was trying to untangle his hand from my hair and remove his penis from my mouth when thankfully things suddenly came to an abrupt stop. No he hadn't come, he had caught and cut his dick on a broken tooth that I had not yet had the chance to go visit the dentist to have fixed. He let my head go and abruptly sat up grabbing his dick and swearing "For fucks sake! What did you do that for?"

Holding his now deflated, sorry looking, blood stained penis he gave me an accusational look. I was dying to laugh, my inappropriate mirth threating to take hold again. OK so it bled a little but it looked worse than it was, blood does that. To hear him carry on you'd have thought I had done a Mrs Bobbitt on him and chopped the sodding thing off. It's a good job men don't have periods, Christ, they'd think they were dying every month.

"I'm so sorry" I said apologetically, biting the inside of my cheek, trying not to grin. I explained about the broken tooth "It was a complete accident. Do you need a bandage? Stitches? Shall I call an ambulance?"

I joked around trying to make light of the situation, it was only a little scratch after all and it soon stopped bleeding but he wasn't in the least bit amused. Apparently he had totally lost his sense of humour along with his erection. He threw on his clothes and stomped off downstairs in a mood. I took that as a hint that he probably would like me to leave.

Poetic justice I thought laughing to myself as I got dressed, my poor clitoris still throbbing against my jeans and not in a good way. It took days for the poor little thing to heal and it's still traumatised by the experience to this day. Needless to say we didn't bother maintaining that particular friendship and I even paid him the ultimate insult of deleting him off Facebook.

So, after the disastrous reacquaintance and accidental but satisfying butchering of my former work colleague's penis, it was back to the dating sites for me. And the dentist.

Joining POF may have been a good move, there were certainly plenty of men to choose from and I was being inundated with messages. No dick pics as yet although I did get one guy who sent me a picture of him in his boxers sporting an obvious healthy erection. He claimed he had both taken and then sent it to me completely by accident. How d'ya manage that then mate?

There was a major downside to POF though. Although the quantity was there the quality just wasn't. 95% of the messages I received were from idiots, weird perverts, they were far too young (only 18 in one case - seriously!), far too old or I simply just didn't fancy them. Some just wanted sex and were quite up-front about that. That was

OK, at least they were honest about their intentions but that wasn't for me. Yes I was looking for some bedroom action but I did want something slightly more meaningful than a fuck and run and especially not with someone already emotionally involved with another.

One of the standard questions when you get chatting with someone is "So what is it you are looking for?" but I had no clue what I was looking for really. I knew I wasn't particularly looking for love or anything serious not at that point anyway I was enjoying my space but if it happened then I wouldn't have any objections. It is I suppose what we are all looking for ultimately but I certainly didn't have an agenda or any expectations on that score. I guess what I was really looking for was chemistry and great sex with someone I could go out and have a laugh with. If I managed to find that and then it developed into something more serious then that would be fine, if not then that would be fine too. It was proving to be an elusive search so far, perhaps I was just being too fussy? No, it's my life and I wasn't going to compromise by settling for just anybody and endure another shit relationship because sometimes I felt lonely.

I narrowed potential dating material down to a handful of possibilities and went on a few more dates but the guys I were meeting either looked nothing like their profile pictures, were rude, turned out to be married or otherwise attached in more than one case or simply just bored me to tears. Some were hopeless, desperate romantics looking for the big L declaring undying love on the first date, gazing adoringly into my eyes and wanting to hold my hand the whole time. Creepy. This genuinely happened to me.

Sad Alistair. We had a lovely date. Just met for a drink, got on well, were both a bit peckish so decided to go for something to eat. Whilst I was hungrily perusing the menu I became aware that he had said something. I looked up to see him staring at me expectantly.

"Sorry, did you say something?" I asked

"Yes. I said I think I love you." he replied

Jesus.

I let out a little laugh "Er, Oh! Thank you?" Probably not the reply he had been hoping for.

"Do you feel the same?" He enquired reaching for my hand and giving me a creepy doe-eyed stare.

"Are you joking around here Alistair?!"

"No, I'm serious." he looked hurt

"We're on a first date. I don't even know if I like you enough for a second date yet, let alone love you!"

"Too soon?" He asked

"Too soon" I agreed. We didn't go on a second date.

I did meet this one guy that I really liked, Andrew. We met for coffee at this trendy new local place that had recently opened and ended up having about seven cups each of strong black Americano, chatting for over four hours about anything and everything. I had caffeine jitters for days. We got on like the proverbial house on fire and I quite fancied him. I got the impression that the feeling was mutual. I'm usually quite good at reading people and why else would a quick coffee last four hours if he didn't like me? The next day I messaged him to thank him for an enjoyable afternoon and being a modern (impatient) woman and quite forward asked him when we could meet for a second date. Maybe my forwardness put him off because puzzlingly he said yes he'd really enjoyed himself too, then ghosted me. Just vanished off the face of the planet like he'd never existed in the first place. Strange and frankly more than a little rude, oh well.

CHAPTER 15

After this particular disappointment dating fatigue hit, hard. I was tired and frankly bored of the whole thing. What was the point? I was just wasting my time here. I was giving serious consideration to giving it all up when I got a match followed by a lovely message from a guy called Liam on Tinder.

Hello there. I've not been on Tinder for several months and had just come on to actually delete my account when your beautiful face popped up. I gave you a swipe right and to my delight we matched! Although you've probably been snapped up by now I'm sending you this message in the hope that you're available for me to take out for dinner in the very near future.

I had liked Liam, giving him a swipe right when I had very first signed up to Tinder, which was several months past, but then promptly forgot all about him when we didn't match.

He was tall, dark and looked fairly handsome on his profile picture, hoping of course that it was recent and genuine. He lived a fair distance from me, about twenty five miles or so which did put me off a little but if we both had cars then that didn't really need to be an issue, it was only a forty minute drive. We exchanged messages for a while and I felt a little bit of excitement building up. Was this, finally, someone who could tick some of the boxes? I tried not to get too carried away with myself, I had been here before after all on more than one occasion.

His profession was a little off-putting, he was an undertaker, but he was articulate, attractive and from what I could tell seemed to be fairly normal, not at all strange. He was certainly very polite, no dick pics, sexual innuendo or trying to convince me to send him pictures of my tits for his wank bank. We hit it off via messaging, quickly progressed to chatting on the phone and got into the habit of speaking almost every day. It took a bit of time to arrange a date around his work commitments, people kept inconveniently dying on the days we arranged dates but our first date turned out to be well worth the wait.

We met in a small quirky town about halfway between where we both lived. He looked just like his profile picture which made a welcome change. He hadn't suddenly aged ten years, lost all his hair or put four stone on. Given his profession I was kind of expecting someone a little solemn, perhaps even a bit on the morbid side but he was fun to be with, polite, intelligent and entertaining.

We had a nice meal in a cute little curry house where the staff were a little over attentive. Can't deny the service was great and the food delicious but after being interrupted and asked for the seventh time if our meal was OK we were starting to get a bit annoyed. Leaving the restaurant we went on to have drinks in a neighbouring bar. We sat chatting and flirting until getting turfed out when they closed at 1am after which we sat in his car kissing like a couple of horny teenagers for another hour or so. We parted with great reluctance, I really, really wanted to go home with him and he did ask but I was sticking to my first date no sex rule. He totally respected my decision and didn't pressure me at all but I've got to admit it was tough to stick to it.

We soon arranged a second date, although it took a good while longer than I would have liked due to his work commitments. Who'd have thought being an undertaker would be so time consuming? Honestly, it was unbelievable the amount of folk inconveniently shuffling off their mortal coils in Yorkshire that summer. I did at one point start to wonder if he was married or otherwise committed, just looking for a bit on the side and using work as an excuse when he couldn't get away from his significant other but he really didn't seem the type. He invited me to his house saying I could stay over if I wanted so it was very unlikely that he lived with someone. Of course I took him up on his offer of staying over,

I was fairly desperate for some good loving and was pinning a lot of hopes on him to be the one to provide that.

I arrived at his place around 7pm on Friday evening as arranged. His home was a little strange, not at all what I was expecting. A quirky little cottage with a beautiful garden full of colourful flowers basking in the summer sunshine and I immediately fell in love with it. Inside was a complete contrast, very dowdy and rather depressing with very old fashioned flowery decor and dark coloured wood. The style was very old lady with the exception of Liam's bedroom which was pure single man. Functional, white walls, black furniture, utilitarian, no frills, very plain. No pictures on the walls apart from a single, large Ikea stock print of New York at night. No ornaments, flowers or cushions, no hints of female influence anywhere.

The rest of the house made sense when he explained he hadn't lived there very long and hadn't had time to get round to decorating it yet. Shamefully, I have to admit, my mind got a little carried away with ideas of how we could decorate the lovely little cottage together until I copped on to myself. Bloody hell, it was only our second date and I was already entertaining fantasies about Sunday morning trips to B&Q together for paint. Imagining scenarios where we would be bickering good naturedly about which furniture we would buy and if we had room for a dishwasher in the quaint but small kitchen. I'd be picking up bridal magazines next!

The evening went really well. We had pizza and beer whilst trying to watch a film that I couldn't really follow because my dirty little mind was elsewhere. We kissed and cuddled up on the sofa and it was so nice to be doing these simple little things that I had missed so much. When the film ended I couldn't wait any longer and although it was still fairly light outside I suggested we go to bed. He actually offered to sleep on the couch if I wanted him to. If I wanted him to? Seriously?! What I wanted him to do was throw me over his shoulder, take me to his bedroom and ravish my body all night. I settled for him holding my hand and leading me up the stairs - well I'm not exactly a lightweight and his staircase was quite narrow so maybe throwing me over his shoulder and carrying me up them was a little ambitious. I was still holding out for the all-night ravishing though. I wish I could tell you that I got the ravishing I was longing for, but sadly not.

We undressed, quite sedately. Him frustratingly taking the time to hang up his clothes and neatly fold, yes fold, his socks and underwear before placing them carefully in his mostly empty washing basket. It was hard for me not to roll my eyes at such behaviour, I mean who on earth folds their dirty laundry?! Takes me all my time to fold my clean laundry. My stuff went, as usual, in a heap on the floor, although noticing he was obviously a bit of a neat freak I did at least make an effort to make it a tidy heap.

He then put on his dressing gown and disappeared to the bathroom. Apparently the fact that he had a woman gagging for sex dressed only in kinky knickers and bra in his bedroom wasn't to stand in the way of his nightly ablutions. He returned after five minutes, offered me a spare dressing gown and said "The bathroom's free." the kinky knickers obviously having zero effect on him. They were going back for a bloody refund.

I obediently donned the dressing gown and trotted off to wash behind my ears, brush my teeth and make sure everything was still clean and fresh in the intimate areas that had been scrubbed to within an inch of their lives, shaved, sprayed and lotioned in anticipation of action three hours earlier. Returning to the bedroom I found him lay in bed - reading a book. At least he was naked I suppose. I had half expected him to be wearing pyjamas, perfectly ironed of course and buttoned up to the neck.

I stood at the side of the bed, clearing my throat to get his attention "Hello! Nearly naked horny woman at your service!"

He looked at me over the top of his reading glasses and raised his eyebrows. Shrugging off the dressing gown and letting it fall to the floor in what I thought was a provocative manner and revealing my sexy new underwear I gave him my best sultry smile. He smiled back. Then said "Would you mind hanging that up for me please, there's a good girl, there's a hook on the back of the door. I'll be with you in a second, just finishing this chapter."

Ohhkayy then.

I'll admit by this point the frustration was starting to get to me and I was feeling rather narky. I slid into bed beside him and lay glaring at the ceiling trying my hardest not to huff and sigh whilst he finished reading *Embalming for Dummies* or whatever. He finally put the book down just as I was beginning to wish I hadn't had a drink so I could just say "Cheerio then!" stomp off to my car and drive home. He pulled me over to him and started to kiss me - finally! I felt his erection growing against my thigh and I had a glimmer of hope that maybe the night wouldn't be a total write off after all.

Sadly though, but perhaps unsurprisingly the sex was disappointing. Text book boring fornication. Missionary position only. Very dissatisfying. The only interesting part was the dirty talk and that was more than a little disconcerting.

His repertoire consisted solely of phrases containing words baby, daddy and cock. He continually referred to himself as "daddy" and me as "baby" saying things like "ride daddy's big cock baby" and "would baby like to sit on daddy's big cock". I wouldn't mind but even despite some not so subtle urging from me, he didn't deviate from missionary the whole time so there was no sitting on and riding of his cock. And OK, whilst a perfectly adequate size he wasn't exactly what I would call big. But I suppose "ride daddy's average sized cock baby" just doesn't have the same ring to it. The daddy thing though was just plain wrong. Admittedly I've never really been very good at dirty talk, mostly it just makes me want to giggle, I was finding it very difficult to keep a straight face.

Of course the second it was over he was back in the bathroom having a shower. I suggested we get in the shower together but he looked at me as if I'd just suggested shitting in his bed. So I showered alone, but at least I was able to crack one off and relieve some of my frustration. I did stay over, didn't really have much choice as I was over the drink drive limit and it was actually quite nice with him spooning me most of the night, oh how I sometimes missed having a man in my bed.

I did hope that maybe the sex would get better over time, perhaps some of my kinky nature might rub off on him and otherwise he did tick quite a few of the perfect boyfriend boxes so we did date for a while. But in addition to the rubbish sex his overly fastidious nature, understandable I suppose given his profession, drove me more than a little bonkers.

My approach to tidying up is to ignore the mess until five minutes before I was due visitors then run around stuffing things in cupboards and drawers like a madwoman on speed. He was the complete opposite, totally anal retentive about everything being in it's place. I can't remember the last time I'd even plugged my iron in but he ironed everything including his socks and underwear. I'd never known anyone, especially a man, like it. Ultimately however it was the continued disappointing, boring, predictable, perfunctory sex that was the deal breaker for me and I called time on the relationship after a few sexually frustrating weeks.

I was getting utterly sick and tired of wasting my time on dates with men then finding the sex was shit, boring or mediocre at best. I enjoy sex and yes I guess some would consider me a little bit kinky but I consider a good, healthy, interesting, varied sex life to be a very important part of a relationship. Of course there are other things that are important in a meaningful relationship. Things like communication, honesty, mutual respect and trust. Having fun and common interests outside the bedroom are important too but even with all these elements in place, if there are no thrills between the sheets then I'm sorry the relationship just doesn't interest me no matter how much of a nice guy he is.

I refuse to ever be a once a week missionary position, lights off keep your nightie on sort of girl. I enjoy slow sensual love making so if he fucks faster than a bunny on speed then it's going to be a no from me. Spare me the rushed, clumsy attempts at foreplay followed by two pumps and a squirt, it's not a race. Why the need for instant gratification? Sure sometimes I enjoy a quick dirty fuck but mostly I like to take my time and enjoy the whole experience. I'm not just looking for a quick orgasm, not that many of those had been forthcoming anyway, I could get as many of those as I wanted by myself, I needed a good lover. I wanted someone to hold me, kiss my neck, pull my hair and smack my arse! Surely there had to be some good lovers somewhere. Where were they all hiding?

CHAPTER 16

Although the sex side of the relationship had been a total disappointment I did miss Liam for a while. It had been nice to have someone to chat to and go places with. To snuggle up to watch TV with. I missed all those everyday little things that couples take for granted and I was lonely for a while but I wasn't willing to compromise too much, been there done that, made me very unhappy. I knew that sadly, he would drive me to insanity before too long. Liam couldn't understand why I had ended the relationship, I hadn't told him it was because of the boring sex I had just said although he was lovely, which indeed in most respects he was I didn't feel like he was the one for me. The old it's not you, it's me, thing. He continued to message me for many months asking for a second chance and telling me how much he missed me. I did have days where I almost gave in but I knew it wouldn't work out in the long run and would just end up in heartache so there was no point. I was feeling fed up and needed a distraction and I found one in the form of Chris. Chris was a perpetually stoned 46 year old teenager who I met on POF. He was actually quite funny and I do like a man who can make me laugh. He was bearded, ginger (or had flowing auburn locks according to his description) not very tall, a bit scruffy, a little chubby. So OK, whilst I would have described his style as missing and although he was not exactly traditionally handsome he was not bad looking either in a cute geeky, short, viking kind of way if you can imagine that. He told me that he played guitar in a band (as did a surprising amount of the men I spoke to) and he sent me some of their music over to have a listen to. It wasn't bad, actually in all fairness it was pretty good, had kind of an 80's metal vibe which I'm rather partial to. We arranged a date to meet Saturday night and he took me out for a curry. We had a great time, I hadn't laughed so much in ages and there was definitely some chemistry there. I felt that here was a man I could let my hair down and have some fun with. When we finished the meal he told me he was skint and was contemplating setting fire to the toilets to cause a distraction whilst we ran away without paying the bill. I think he was only half joking. In any case he did manage to pay and I was very relieved because I was wearing heels that I could barely walk in never mind run and I didn't have enough cash on me to cover the bill.

A few days later he invited me over to his place for a takeaway. He didn't drive but I was happy to drive over to him to see him as I had enjoyed his company the first time we met. He omitted to tell me during our many conversations that he lived with his elderly mother, but I did find it a little suspicious when he ushered me straight up the stairs to his bedroom muttering something like the downstairs telly was on the blink. His bedroom was a bit of a shocker. Now I'm a bit messy, I can always think of a hundred more important and interesting things to do than clean my house, but this was ridiculous. I think he was going for an early nineties, seriously can't be arsed, adolescent style. Whilst I'm far from being a snob I can't say I was enthralled with the idea of being entertained in that dump of a bedroom complete with overflowing ashtrays, dirty crockery and nasty, suspiciously stiff socks and towels all over the floor. I was a little less than impressed to be honest by his massive collection of video games, posters Blu-tacked to the wall and most especially by the fragrant, unwashed bedding. Seriously, the smell of sheets that haven't been washed for weeks isn't exactly a turn on and although he had opened the window and lit a scented candle it did nothing to mask the unpleasant odour. I thought he could have bothered to make an effort to clean up before I'd arrived but then it occured to me that perhaps he had, maybe this was what passed for clean and tidy in his mind. He was the complete opposite to OCD Liam.

I sat gingerly on the edge of the single (well it was a small room) bed wondering how long to stay before making my excuses and leaving. Chris, stoned, was totally oblivious to my discomfort and disgust. He got his guitar out and started to mock serenade me, doing a stupid dance. He played really well and his singing wasn't too bad either. He made me laugh and to my surprise I actually found I was starting to relax and enjoy myself. He was very entertaining. I decided to stay for a while, it's not as if I had anything more interesting to do. We ordered pizza which I paid for, indeed he was skint, his usual financial state as it turned out but he had paid for the previous meal so I didn't mind, I would have offered anyway. I did find the amount of marijuana he smoked a little disturbing. I've nothing against weed but he smoked it almost incessantly, no wonder he was so laid back. And permanently skint. After eating the pizza we ended up rolling around on the bed a little, on top of the covers (there was no way I was getting under those stinking sheets). It had been a while since I'd had sex and I was feeling a little relaxed and horny, probably from passive smoking all that weed. It was a very warm night, we soon worked up a sweat and stripped off. Sex with Chris was surprisingly pretty good and it was fun. He wasn't particularly well endowed but he knew what to do with it, had a great technique and certainly had plenty of stamina. He could literally go for hours, probably something to do with the cannabliss he was constantly smoking. He was that stoned frankly it was amazing that he could even get an erection.

He asked me if I liked to receive oral sex. In all honestly it's not something I particularly enjoy, I'm always worried that I'm not clean enough or that I may have an accidental botty cough. It's happened once or twice, kind of ruins the romance. Also I don't tend to climax from it so it always feels like too much worry and effort for little return but he was kind of insistent about it, assuring me that he had a very skillful tongue and was very keen to demonstrate his talent. I told him to go ahead and he enthusiastically buried his head between my thighs. He did indeed have a gifted tongue, complemented by an interesting finger technique. I tried to relax and was finally getting into the rhythm, starting to enjoy it, thinking that I might actually get an orgasm out of it, just reaching the point of no return, that blissful feeling building and building, when in burst his bloody mother to say goodnight.

I didn't know who was more mortified. There was me, lay in all my sweaty, naked glory just about to climax, Chris's head buried between my legs, his naked arse up in the air and poor old Betty got a right eyeful. Embarrassed I grabbed for a (suspiciously crispy) towel to try to cover myself with whilst his mother made a funny kind of squeaking noise and backed out of the room at a speed that was frankly astonishing for a little old lady. Chris jumped up angrily shouting "MUM - for fucks SAKE!"

Despite this rather shaky start I did start to see Chris on a fairly regular basis, nothing serious just a bit of fun friends with benefits kind of arrangement. He was good fun albeit in an adolescent kind of way that was unless he was on one of his frequent downers. When he was on one of those I wouldn't hear from him for weeks and just when I thought I'd heard the last of him he would send me a message.

He had apologised for not telling me about living with his mum and explained he was living back there after his divorce, which I found out later was nine years previously, obviously he was in no hurry to get a place of his own. I think after seeing him for a while he was beginning to entertain ideas of moving in with me. Oh no, I didn't think so.

After a couple of months he told me he was falling for me and asked me if I'd like to be his girlfriend, go exclusive, stop seeing other people. Sadly I didn't even have to think about this. There was no way I would ever entertain anything serious with him. He was sweet and funny and good in bed and I liked him a lot and cared about him but he was also apathetic and lazy. For goodness sake he couldn't even be bothered making the effort to put clean sheets on his bed and picking up his dirty clothes off the floor when he knew I was going over. Perpetually stoned, he wasn't very good at maintaining relationships or gainful employment and was frequently out of work. He couldn't drive, had never learned so I always had to go to him and we never went anywhere other than his bedroom.

Whilst seeing Chris I was also seeing Pete who I also met on POF. Told you I was a greedy girl. In fairness I knew things would never be serious with Chris so I was just keeping my options open and both of them knew I was dating other men.

Pete was the polar opposite of Chris, couldn't have been more different. Tall, dark haired, good looking (although nowhere near as good looking as he thought he was). Driven, focused, confident with a high flying career he was a great kisser a snappy dresser and wore fantastic shoes. He was very, very good in bed, had a nice sized penis and always made sure I was satisfied before he came himself. Pity then he was such an absolute cock-womble.

Pete was the epitome of the eternal bachelor. As far as I could gather, never in his 42 years had he had a serious relationship. Apart from our first date where we met in a pub, he never took me out anywhere. Whilst perfectly happy to shag me stupid, the only ladies his type would be seen out in public with were arm candy girls. Stick thin, glamorous Barbie blondes. Fake tan, fake nails, fake eyelashes, fake eyebrows, fake boobs, fake hair, fake lips, fake laugh, fake orgasm. The type that spend a fortune and far too much time and effort in my opinion on their appearance and designer outfits. Slightly chubby girls who only wore make-up on special occasions, had disobedient hair, shopped at Primarni and actually dared enjoyed themselves when they went out getting stupidly pissed and singing badly on karaoke were good for fucking but not for dating.

It was obvious from the start that our relationship was just that of fuck buddies. He would think nothing of sending me a message saying "Thinking of you" with a close up photo of his erect pecker and a winking emoji at 1am, followed by a message asking me if I wanted to go over. Early am booty call requests I always denied, strangely the dick pics failed to make me feel all warm and fuzzy inside and didn't make me want to rush over to be with him. Occasionally he would balance these out with cute little pictures of couples holding hands or some other corny shit he'd screenshot off Facebook and probably sent to all the female contacts in his phonebook. That was his only occasional effort at romance.

Sex with Pete, although very good (I wouldn't have put up with him otherwise), was for one reason only and that was to get our mutual rocks off. Although he did always make sure I was satisfied I doubt he ever had the least bit of genuine interest in my pleasure. The fact he wanted to make me climax was probably more out of concern for his reputation and to keep me interested in seeing him. There was never any post-coital cuddling or conversation. Never any question of my staying over.

After he came he would jump up with alarming alacrity, smack my arse, tell me to go put the kettle on and then he'd go get in the shower. After his shower, he would put the football / rugby / golf on the telly and ignore me until I said I was leaving. He would then give me a quick peck on the cheek, say "That was ace darlin, thanks" usher me out of the door and not even bother texting or ringing to check I'd got home alright. See? Total cockwomble.

Often there would be weeks when I didn't hear anything from him at all. He must have been having some luck with one of the girls higher up on the booty list pecking order when he wasn't messaging me. In truth, I couldn't have cared less. It was what it was, a mutually agreed sharing of each other's bodies for the purpose of sexual gratification. Nothing more. I never developed any feelings for him and was certainly never going to be doing any chasing after him.

CHAPTER 17

It was the second week in July and summer was fulfilling its promise for a change by actually being summery. Boy it was hot, the fan was doing overtime and I would go for a drive in my car just so I could bask in the lovely cold air con. Not that I was complaining, far from it. I was enjoying what has got to be one of, if not the best perk of working from home which was sitting with the laptop in the garden basking in the sunshine topping up my tan, occasionally even doing a bit of work.

Things got even hotter when I got a temporary new neighbour. The owner of the house and my usual neighbour, Alfie, spent most of his time away in sunnier climates or on cruises enjoying his favourite pastime of hunting for well preserved rich widows of a certain age and often let his house out on Airbnb. One of life's proper characters, Alfie was a widowed, dapper, retired dentist somewhere in his late seventies although he looked and acted a good twenty years younger and would only admit to being sixty something. His favourite saying was "There's plenty of lead in the old pencil yet, Viagra not necessary!"

You would often find him a little tipsy down in the local pub or corner shop chatting up the widows, divorcees and landlady with his cheeky banter, holding court with some of the wild and colourful (and I suspect somewhat embellished) stories of his misspent youth. He was often totally inappropriate but as he was so cute and cheeky and meant no harm he got away with it. Although the ladies pretend to be appalled by him and his ways, secretly they basked in his attention and rumour had it he had had more than one fling with some of the more desirable local ladies he tipped his hat at. If the ladies at the Wednesday knit and natter group in the church hall had fallen out you could almost guarantee Alfie had something to do with it, he certainly inspired the green eyed monster.

He often invited me over for dinner when he was at home or he would come to me and I always thoroughly enjoyed his company. We would have copious amounts of wine and he would entertain me for hours with his stories. Upon leaving he would give me a big hug and a smacker right on the lips and sigh "If only I was twenty years younger, the things I would do to you, you sexy girl!"

As much as I loved Alfie I have to say the newbie was much easier on the eye. He was actually under retirement age, very good looking with a body I wanted to cover with Ben & Jerry's finest then leisurely lick clean. After employing some of my probably not so subtle investigating I discovered he was alone, from America and staying for four weeks. My sex radar pinged with interest. I actually started to make a bit of an effort with my appearance brushing my hair in the mornings, wearing a little make-up and I dug out my pretty little floral sundresses rather than slobbing around in the denim shorts and oversized mens t-shirts I usually favoured. The locals kept raising their eyebrows at my appearance and asking me if I was going to a wedding or had a job interview.

I nodded a casual hello to the hot newbie in passing a couple of times, nonchalantly sauntering past going on pretend walks to nowhere, sneaking around the back, back to my house when I was sure he wasn't looking. Wearing my darkest sunnies so I could sneakily eye up his delicious, half naked body which he often conveniently displayed on a sunlounger in the front garden. Thank goodness we had sun for him to lounge in for a change. I gave him a few days to settle in - didn't want to seem too keen - then invited him over for coffee one morning. He accepted my invitation with a thank you spoken in a lazy American drawl, flashing a knowing grin that revealed a perfect set of teeth and a couple of cute dimples. Major fanny flutters.

The next morning at nine am prompt there was a knock on the door and there he stood in all his

tall, well proportioned, tanned, gorgeous man-
liness. He was smiling that lovely smile with a
twinkle in his blue eyes and holding a bottle of
freshly squeezed orange juice. Cue more flutters
in the nether regions. I invited him in and over a
glass of juice got to know him a little better.

His name was Connor, a Phys Ed Coach,
(why does that sound so much sexier than gym
teacher?) a little younger than me in his late
thirties. He had come over to England for a few
weeks to get over a break up. He'd been married
nine years and his divorce had just come through.
He told me he had caught her cheating on him
but he seemed very equable about this fact, no
bitterness or nastiness in his voice when he was
telling me about it. He had a feel good, relaxed
but motivated vibe about himself that was infec-
tious and made a change from the usual dowdy
depressing nature of a lot of people I met. Even
Walter liked him and Walter liked no-one, I suspected not even me, he only put up with me because I fed him.

It was nice for a change when he showed genuine interest in me, my life, my job, my friends
and family. A vast majority of the men I had been
on dates with either never bothered to ask anything about me or quite obviously only feigned
interest, their eyes glazing over when I spoke
about myself. He fired about a million questions
at me about my upbringing, the village I lived
in, English customs and we whiled away a pleas-

ant morning chatting about all kinds of random subjects. He thought our schools quaint and old-fashioned with our uniforms and traditions and he roared with laughter at some of my tales of the stupid scrapes I had gotten myself into and some of the strange dates I had been on lately.

It was almost lunch time, I was starving and had lots of work I should have been getting on with but didn't want him to go because I was enjoying his company too much. I put the kettle on and offered him a biscuit. He said he didn't really eat sugar and carbs but to go ahead if I wanted one, winking at me and telling me he liked a lady with a bit of meat on her bones. His wife, he told me had been in great shape but her body was just so hard, he liked to cuddle something soft. I think it was meant as a compliment. I made the drinks, came back into the living room with the mugs, coffee for me, green tea for him and almost spat out the remnants of the ginger nut I had hurriedly stuffed into my gob in the kitchen when I noticed he was sat on my sofa wearing nothing but that lovely grin and an impressive hard on.

Now, part of me thought that really I should be appalled and outraged at this forwardness, this assumption that I wanted his body, the arrogance of the man! I should be insulted and offended that he would presume I would be so easy. But then I thought ah fuck it, I did want his body why pretend otherwise, why play games? We were both consenting, horny adults and here was a genuine

Adonis offering me, this forty something average looking, slightly chubby woman, his delightful body. I'd be mad to turn him down. I carefully placed the mugs on the coffee table and off up to the bedroom we went for a few hours of very pleasurable fun and frolicks.

Oh, oh, oh! He was gooood. Slightly bossy, which I love in a man. In a gentle but firm tone that invited no arguments he ordered me to take off my clothes and stand in front of him. Trembling a little I did as I was told. I stood naked whilst he took his time looking at my body. I was a little uncomfortable under his scrutiny trying to hold my stomach in, my hands covering the flabby little fold that was left after the weight loss. He gently took hold of my hands, moved them away and kissed the parts of me that I hated the most. "Don't hide" he said "You are beautiful"

My immediate reaction was to snort with laughter and tell him he didn't need to give me his bullshit, that I was a sure shag but when I looked at his face I saw his desire and longing and thought, wow! I think he actually means it. He took my hand and pulled me over to the bed. We lay on our sides facing each other and kissed with alternate gentleness and passion for what felt like forever, our hands ceaselessly exploring each other's bodies. Finally he pushed me onto my back and got on top of me not stopping the kissing and slowly slid inside of me.

It was heavenly.

He took his time varying his thrusts, getting faster and faster until I was on the edge of orgasm then maddeningly stopping. He would wait a moment or two before starting again. Four or five times he did this to me until I was insane with desire and begging him not to stop before finally letting me reach a sweet, sweet, long climax him coming at the same time.

After I got my breath back I asked him if all American men were so good in bed. "Of course, sex ed is a major part of our curriculum" he replied, then asked with a cheeky grin "Are all English ladies so friendly?"

We had an amazing time that summer, it was one of the best summers of my life. We spent a lot of time together both in and out of bed. I knew that in reality he was only using me, there would be no happily ever after, it was just a holiday romance, a rebound relationship there was no real love there but those few weeks were not about reality it was pure fantasy. That was totally fine by me. I was happy to go along for the ride and I thoroughly enjoyed it for what it was. I was happy to be his tour guide, friend, companion and lover for those few blissful weeks in that long hot summer.

CHAPTER 18

And God said "I will put these wonderful things in the bodies of my creations"

"Excellent, what shall we call them?"

"Hormones"

"Wonderful. What will these hormones do"

"They will make the males virile and strong"

"Of course. And the females?"

"They will make them moody, unpredictable, unreasonable, irrational and fat"

One particular day I was feeling particularly tetchy. Moody and out of sorts I didn't have a clue what was wrong with me, I put it down to hormones, although it wasn't like me to be hormonal.

I was munching on a Jaffa cake whilst catching up on some work. I had eaten seventy two in the space of two days. Seventy two! Six packets! It was Asda's fault, they were on a three for two offer and I could never resist a bargain. Problem was, I didn't even like Jaffa cakes. Never had liked anything orange flavoured. I didn't like prawns either, well that was until just recently when I had decided they were my new favourite food.

Mmm...

I stopped working and started musing about my new favourite foods. Perhaps I was pregnant? At my age? Don't be silly. Mind you, I hadn't gone through the menopause yet, that joy was still probably a few years away, so I guess it could happen. A woman I had been at school with had had a baby last year. It certainly wasn't an impossibility.

I thought back, had I had any unprotected sex? There was that one night a few weeks ago with Chris where we had gotten a little drunk and carried away and not used a condom but I had a coil fitted and it wasn't due to be changed for another - shit! I should have had it changed about eight months ago.

Oh my God. I felt sick. Nausea. Another symptom. Panic stricken I considered my breasts, yes they had been a little sore, were they bigger? I felt them, didn't think so, maybe just a little.... Shit, shit SHIT! I couldn't have another child, not at my age and not with someone as feckless as Chris.

I consulted the font of all knowledge, Alexa. "Alexa - what are the chances of getting pregnant at age 43?"

Alexa told me "The chances of a flea infestation in the home increase when you have domestic animals with fur such as cats and dogs"

"Oh fuck off Alexa you useless piece of shite"

I opened my laptop and asked a medical expert - Doctor Google. Doctor Google confirmed what I already knew, that it was unlikely I would conceive naturally at my age but not impossible and shared links to several heartwarming stories about women my age and above who had conceived naturally which I read through with increasing panic. Most of these women were over the moon to be pregnant in their forties, were they mad? Heartwarming though some of these stories were they did nothing to improve my mood or calm my panic stricken mind.

I was seeing Connor that night. Was it morally acceptable to have sex with someone when you were carrying someone else's baby I wondered. I told myself not to be so bloody silly, I was NOT pregnant.

I messaged my sister

> Hiya. Guess what? I ate 72 Jaffa cakes in two days!!!!

Greedy bitch ! lol x

> Thing is, I don't even like Jaffa cakes

Oh.... Are you pregnant???! xx

I was absolutely and totally unfairly awful to Connor that night. He kept asking me what was wrong but I could hardly tell him I thought I might be pregnant to someone else now could I? We had sex and I'm sure it was amazing as always but I was only there in body. My mind was elsewhere having a nervous breakdown.

"Babe?" said Connor as we lay snuggled up together afterwards.

"Don't. Fucking. Call. Me. That!" I growled at him in a scary low voice

"Call you what?" he looked at me puzzled

"Babe!"

"But I always call you Babe" he pointed out.

"Yes! I know" I replied "But I have got. A fucking. NAME!!"

"Erm, OK, sorry bay.. errr Scarlett. I was just wondering if I could have some of those Jaffa Cakes?"

"No, you fucking well can NOT!!" I shouted both to his astonishment and mine then burst into ugly tears.

The next morning I did six pregnancy tests. All negative. Relieved, I booked into the family planning clinic to have my coil changed with some urgency. Luckily I managed to get an appointment two days later.

"Oh, you're a little late with this." the doctor pointed out peering at the computer screen at my notes "Have you had any unprotected sex?"

"Erm, yes." I mumbled, looking at my feet blushing and feeling like an irresponsible, promiscuous, teenager.

"OK Kokie then" she said smiling patronisingly at me and offering me a little plastic pot "Go do me a little wee, we'll just do a quick pregnancy test before we continue."

"I'm not pregnant" I assured her "I did a couple of tests already."

"Let's just make doubly sure shall we? Those home tests are not always 100% accurate."

Of course it was negative. I hadn't expected it not to be but it was still a relief to have it confirmed beyond all doubt. My symptoms, the doctor explained, were probably down to the coil, which was impregnated with hormones, coming to the end of it's life and causing me to have premenstrual symptoms for the first time in years. I thanked the Gods for not blessing me with a feckless ginger baby. Got me a shiny new coil and apologised to Connor for being a woman with out of control hormones but he just laughed and hugged me.

Almost every morning Connor would call over with fresh juice, fruit or delicious pastries from Penny's bakery. His no carb, no sugar diet going out of the window, will-power crumbling when faced with such tantalisingly tasty home baked goodies. He loved all the country pubs the homemade food, pints of real ale. We made sure we got plenty of sexercise to work off all the extra calories. I lost inches off my thighs, a result of the amount of time I spent with my legs wrapped around his back. We went to the beach one day where we got caught in a sudden heavy downpour sheltering in a cave where we ended up making love, almost getting caught by an elderly lady walking her dog who also sought shelter from the rain. Luckily the yelps from her overly excited Labrador warned us of her presence before she saw us in our compromising position. We couldn't keep our hands off each other, we were like a couple of sex mad teens.

We were highly compatible sexually. I can't explain how or why but our bodies just seemed to fit right. I was finally getting the sensual, satisfying love making I had been craving and crammed in as much as I could get but sadly, all too soon, the fantasy had to end and it was time for him to go back to the USA.

I had frequently counselled myself not to fall in love with Connor, I knew it was just a holiday romance, but it was still with a very heavy heart that I dropped him off at the airport on a suitably grey Thursday morning. We had one another's numbers of course but we made no promises to keep in touch, both old enough to know that once reality bit, life would just get in the way of those promises no matter how meaningful. We hugged for the last time. I squeezed him as hard as I could breathing in his unique smell, committing that and the feel of his beautiful body to my memory. Laughing he prised my body off him

"You're gonna squeeze the breath right out of me! Sorry, but I'm gonna miss my plane, I got to go."

I nodded at him. I couldn't speak past the huge lump that had formed in my throat and tears were threatening. He kissed me one last time then stood back, his hands on my shoulders. Looking at me with that gorgeous grin, he winked, let go of my shoulders, picked up his bag, said "Take care babe" and then he was gone.

CHAPTER 19

Hey. I'm looking for a hot wife. Interested?

Thanks for the compliment but I'm not really looking for marriage!

Suggest you Google hot wife

Googles hot wife   oh!

Despite repeatedly telling myself not to fall in love with Connor my emotional heart never did heed my slightly more pragmatic mind which is why I had made a complete tit of myself more than once in the name of love.

I was heartbroken for a while after he went home. I wandered around bereft for a couple of weeks not knowing what to do with myself. Occupying myself with stupid daydreams in which Connor would come to the realisation that he couldn't live without me, jump on a plane, come back to England and knock on my door declaring undying love. My heart jumped every time

I had an unexpected visitor stupidly hoping it would be him. I even entertained ideas of going over to America, just turning up at the airport. I played these alternate fantasy scenarios over and over in my mind with slight variations but which would always end with us throwing ourselves into each other's arms with tears of joy and living happily ever after.

Sadly though, this was real life not some corny Hollywood romcom or far fetched chick lit and I knew the likely outcome would be far removed from the fantasy. Besides America was a big place with lots of airports and I didn't have a clue where he lived. Best to leave well alone and savour the memories of the near perfect few weeks we had spent together. We did keep in touch via messenger for a little while but it was just too painful, the messages becoming less intimate, more polite and so I eventually just let the contact fade away.

Jill came to visit one afternoon a couple of weeks after Connor left, bursting in unannounced in her usual hyperactive manner to find me slumped unhappily at the kitchen table with my laptop open "Afternoon, I've bought you a present" she said with a wink, shoving a black plastic bag in my direction.

"It's a magic wand." she explained as I took the bag and looked inside to discover something that definitely had not been a prop in a Harry Potter film. "Make sure you lie on a towel if you're going to crack one off using it. That big boy will make you squirt for sure unlike most of those dickless wonders you've been meeting up with."

Most people gifted you flowers or wine or chocolate. Not Jill, no, she gave you sex toys. She knew I was missing Connor and this was her effort at trying to cheer me up. Even though she was a staunch feminist lesbian that usually berated most men as being utter arseholes even she had liked Connor and been seduced by his good looks, sunny nature and infinite good humour.

"Don't ever repeat this, and if you do I'll deny ever saying it" she had whispered to me one evening after a few glasses of wine "I don't fuck boys, but if you hadn't already lay claim to that beautiful person I would ride him for hours without a second thought the horny bastard."

I mumbled my thanks for the gift.

"Plugs in, runs off the mains. Will save you a fortune in batteries whilst you're looking for your next shag hero" she explained. Then with a sympathetic nature and concern totally unlike her usual self she looked at me and asked how I was.

"Craving dick but totally unwilling to deal with men to get some" I answered sulkily. "I mean look at this, this guy wants a hot wife, do you know what that is. It's basically a woman he can pimp out to other guys whilst he watches her get shagged. That's how he gets his rocks off!"

"Fucking perve. You could try women?" she suggested as if sexuality was something you could just choose like a new pair of shoes "You love boobs."

"I do love boobs" I agreed.

I do love boobs and all their lovely, rounded soft bounciness but more in an admiring them from afar with an occasional bit of boob envy kind of way, not in a sexual one.

"I just don't think sex with women is my cup of coffee" I said "I don't particularly like receiving oral and the idea of me doing any muffin munching in return just turns my stomach. Sorry."

"Jesus!" Jill shouted (she liked to include the neighbours in our conversations) "we lezzers don't just go down on each other you know!"

This I did know, as now did the rest of the street. She would often and in great detail tell me stories of her sexual exploits with whoever was her girlfriend at the time. Some of the stuff she got up to was shocking but admirably inventive. Her orgasm tally, both giving and receiving, was definitely much higher than mine.

"We could find you a big butch type with an amazing pair of tits who would get off by rogering you stupid with an enormous strap on. Best of both worlds." She said looking in my biscuit tin. "Jesus, you've no decent biscuits in here." she complained.

I gestured towards the cupboard where there were 12 packets of Jaffa cakes gathering dust. Now my new coil had been in place for a few weeks and my hormones restored to their previous sane levels I hated them again.

"Urgh, Jaffa cakes, no thanks." She said "I'll go to the shop for some chocolate hobnobs."

"Please don't mention knobs!" I cried

On the positive side I certainly had been enjoying a veritable sex feast that summer after the famine earlier in the year. I still had the two friends with benefits relationships on the go with Chris and Pete but I knew that they were never going to develop into anything more serious. The sex was OK, even good most of the time which was the only reason why I bothered to keep seeing them. However, one of them was a bipolar, immature stoner and the other a complete tosser who considered himself to be God's gift to women so those relationships were never going to be anything other than an occasional boredom shag.

I decided to get back on the dating scene with the hopes of finding something a little more meaningful or at least distract myself from missing Connor. Up to now meaningful relationships were being quite elusive but I had previously been having fun looking so why not get back out there? I was young (ish), free and technically single after all.

Logging on to the dating sites for the first time in weeks, I found I had quite a few messages. One was a picture message from a guy called Tom with a short message

`Hey, remember me? xx`

I vaguely recalled chatting to him some months back but couldn't really remember all that much about him. He did have a very nice body. His message went on to say

`Sorry I've not been in touch I had to go to prison for a while and they wouldn't let me go on POF while I was inside ha ha!`

I looked back at the picture of a ripped looking Tom in gym shorts (nice body obviously been working out whilst incarcerated) and noticed he was sporting HMP's latest fashion accessory on his left ankle. I asked what he'd been in prison for. Nothing much, just a spot of aggravated burglary. Next.

I met and had a few dates with Stephen who at 54 was a good few years older than me. He was a lovely guy, insisted on picking me up and spoiling me with flowers and lovely meals out. Things were going great until, yes you guessed it, it got to the sex. The first time was great, apart from the fact he went as red as a beetroot and I was very concerned that he was going to have a stroke or something. "Oh don't worry" he reassured me when I commented on his alarming colour "I've just forgotten to take my blood pressure medication, I'll be fine"

A few days later we had been out for a few drinks then gone back to his place for a nightcap. Things were getting steamy in the bedroom and

I was giving him one of my legendary blow jobs. All was going well, he was obviously enjoying himself judging by the noises of appreciation he was making when all of a sudden he went quiet. Then limp, his erection deflating faster than a popped balloon. I looked up and noticed he was unconscious. I panicked, my heart stopping for a moment. I honestly thought I'd killed him with my amazing oral skills but with enormous relief I realised he was still breathing. When he regained consciousness he was very blasé about the whole thing, laughing it off and telling me it happened all the time but I found it very disconcerting and just couldn't carry on seeing him after that. I was too scared of finishing him off, death by blow job, not something that I particularly wanted on my record. I suppose at least he'd have gone with a smile on his face.

Steering clear of the older guys after the worrying experience with Stephen I then had a couple of dates with Jake who was quite a bit younger than me. We had a brilliant first date and a few days later he invited me over to his place. I accepted his invitation and he cooked me a lovely dinner going all out to impress me. The meal was delicious, garlic mushrooms, perfectly cooked steak served with salad and then a rich chocolate mousse for dessert. After food we half watched a film having a bit of a kiss and a cuddle on the couch. We had a lovely evening but although he was a very attractive guy and great company I disappointingly found I wasn't really feeling turned on. It was actually becoming somewhat of an effort to kiss this gorgeous guy. What on earth was going on? What was wrong with me? I should have been gagging for it! I was hopeful that things might improve, I did find him attractive so surely there had to be some chemistry? When Jake suggested we go up to his bedroom I happily agreed having a quiet but firm word with my libido as I trotted up the stairs behind him.

We got up to his very pleasant, neat and tidy bedroom where the cutest little black kitten was curled up asleep on his bed. He went to shoo the kitten away and me, being a bit of a crazy cat lady, went a bit gaga over the little furball and asked him not to. I then spent a good while stroking and playing with it totally forgetting about poor Jake. After several minutes he gave me a polite reminder that he was there by loudly clearing his throat. I looked up to find him standing naked in front of me with an impressive hard on. I think he wanted me to be stroking and playing with something other than the cat. Oops! I reluctantly left the little kitty alone, got undressed and got into bed with Jake.

We carried on where we had left off with the kissing and cuddling for a while but then we just stopped and looked at each other. Despite getting off to what had appeared to be a great start

there wasn't actually any sexual chemistry between us at all. I had zero fanny flutters and by
the fact that he now had a sad, wilted willy I
was guessing Jake just wasn't feeling it either. We
mutually agreed it wasn't working. He was quite
pleasant, polite and matter of fact about it, as if
it happened to him all the time, maybe it did.
Maybe he had dud pheromones or something.

 We ended up getting dressed and I went home totally confused about what had just happened. At
least I'd been fed a very nice steak dinner. It was
altogether a very strange experience, the first
and last time I went to bed with an attractive
guy, didn't have sex but played with his pussy!

CHAPTER 20

*Hi gorgeous, fancy meeting up? I'm 18
and really into older women xxxxxxx*

*Bugger off Jason, you're barely legal
and I have underwear older than you*

One thing I was finding quite surprising on the dating sites was the amount of younger men interested in older women. I had several messages from boys a lot younger than me. Some were ridiculously young, young enough to be my son in some cases, not my cup of coffee at all. There is a difference between a cougar and a cradle snatcher and I was not interested in being the latter.

I did go on dates with one or two who were quite a few years younger than me though. A few years was fine, I do consider myself to be quite young at heart anyway, most people my age seem so old! In general though what I found with the much younger guys, was that we tended not to have anything in common and as I had sadly found with Jake there wasn't really any sexual chemistry. So when I met Mark, being a good ten years younger than me, I was very surprised that I found myself getting along particularly well with him.

He was very much the gentleman, attentive, good looking, intelligent and in great shape. We went on a couple of dates which I thoroughly enjoyed, we appeared to have a lot in common, conversation flowed, there was definitely chemistry there and I found myself looking forward to seeing him again.

It was our third date and again we had a really good time. We went out for a meal and Mark was, as always, the perfect gentleman, respectful, considerate and well mannered. I had already decided that if the date went well and it seemed like he would be agreeable I would invite him back to mine. I had even gone to the trouble of picking up the dirty washing off the bathroom floor, changing the sheets and putting some candles in the bedroom before I came out in anticipation of the possibility of a bit of romance.

After we had eaten I suggested we go back to mine for a nightcap. With a knowing grin he enthusiastically agreed and I tingled with the anticipation of the possibility of a good energetic sex session.

We kissed a little in the taxi on the way home and he whispered in my ear that he had a big dick and it was all for me. This got me more excited.

As you've probably gathered I am a greedy girl and I do like a well endowed man but I did start to wonder if I'd made a bit of a mistake when he pounced on me and started to try to drag my tits out of the top of my dress whilst we were still in the cab. Easy tiger, I thought, moving his hand away, plenty of time for that later, no need to be giving the driver an eyeful. The driver was definitely watching the proceedings with lots of interest through the rear view mirror with no shame and not paying enough attention to the road for my liking.

 We got back to mine and he got straight down to business no messing about here with drinks and small talk. Kissing me so hard our teeth banged together he then pushed me up against the wall grabbed my hand he shoved it down the front of his trousers. He was seriously disillusioned, he definitely did not have a big dick. He didn't even have an average size one. It was literally the size of my finger, girth and length. In the sausage world it would qualify somewhere between a cocktail and a chipolata. I must admit I was very disappointed and almost sent him home there and then for false advertising.

OK, so dick size isn't everything maybe he could make up for it with technique, fingers, tongue? Early indications were not favourable. The gentlemanly demeanor had most certainly vanished, he'd left that behind at the restaurant. With a distinct lack of courtesy he shoved me up against the wall viciously yanking down the top of my dress and bra exposing my tits. He grabbed at them, pulling and twisting like he was trying to yank them right off my body and then bit my nipples, hard enough to leave bruises the next day.

Before I got the chance to object to this rough approach, he changed direction quickly pushing up my skirt and rubbing his fingers hard against my crotch. I think he was trying to find my clitorus. Just as I was about to push him away and tell him to stop he shoved his fingers into my mouth and ordered "Suck them bitch".

Jesus, someone had been watching far too much bad porn. I tried to push him away but he was not finished with his brutal approach to loving. He grabbed my hair hard, yanked my head back, called me a fucking naughty girl, asked me if I had any toys and whether I took it up the arse whereupon I came to the swift conclusion that it was time for him to go home.

Predictably he was not very impressed when I called time out and told him he had to leave. He pushed me back up against the wall grinding his groin into my stomach and asking in all seriousness how could I not want this big boy inside me. Erm, well no thanks, it's just too much meat for me to handle? Seriously, it was very difficult not to laugh in his face and tell him to fuck right off but as the situation was unpredictable I decided to stay polite but firm saying in a tone that invited no argument that I was sorry but I'd made a mistake he was not for me and I would prefer it if he left. Immediately. Right now.

He really was not happy and told me in all seriousness that I was going to suck him off. He still had hold of my hair and tried to force my head down towards his crotch. I was done being polite and I ordered him to take his fucking hands off me. Luckily he did as I asked without me having to resort to violence and knee him hard in the bollocks.

He tried one last ditch attempt, what about a hand job he whined, because how could I make him leave with that massive hard on? Really? I assured him no one would notice. He glared at me, he was angry but there was no way I was being pressured into having what would definitely be shit sex, or otherwise giving any sexual favours to this man.

I was wary of what he may be capable of, he was taller and stronger than me and I did have some concerns for a moment that the situation could get worse, spiraling completely out of control and I could end up hurt. Regardless, I stood my ground, no negotiations, no backing down. Without further hesitation, I called a taxi and sent him on his way making him wait outside for the car. He told me I was a prick tease as he stomped out and informed me that he didn't want to see me again.

Can't say I was overly heartbroken about that.

I must admit I was more than a little shaken by the experience with Mark, things could have ended up a lot nastier than they turned out and it did put me off dating for a while. However, I reasoned with myself that out of all the dates I had been on this was the only time I had felt threatened like that and that I mustn't let it put me off. Stupidly I had become a little too complacent about my personal safety, I might be in my forties but I was still as much at risk as a younger woman so I made sure I was in contact with a friend at certain prearranged intervals whilst on dates from then onwards and that someone knew where I was and who I was with at all times. Important to stay safe.

CHAPTER 21

It was a Friday night, a few weeks after the doomed evening with Mark. Another weekend of being a sad lonely singleton with no sex life. I had no more dates planned, to be honest the past couple of experiences had put me off and I had kind of lost interest for the time being. The whole thing was feeling too much like hard work it just wasn't fun any more. I hadn't been interested in seeing any of my friends with benefits lately either. Chris was in the middle of one of his frequent depressive just leave me alone to get stoned and morbid episodes and frankly I couldn't be arsed with Pete's arrogant fuckery so had just been settling for playing with my friends with batteries instead. Much less effort.

I didn't fancy staying in on my lonesome and it was mad Paddy's karaoke night at the local which was always good for a laugh so I met up with a couple of friends to have a warble and a few beverages.

I was entertaining, or probably more accurately, vocally abusing the poor punter's ears with my version of Hanky Panky. I'm not the world's best singer, far from it, actually I can't sing for shit, but what I lack in technical singing ability I sure more than make up for with enthusiasm, especially after a drink or three. Just as I was telling everyone how much I like to be treated like a bad girl, in through the door walked the leading man in many a sexual fantasy of mine. No, not Orlando Bloom, although he has starred in a couple - strangely as his Lord of The Rings character Legolas. Weird, I know, I can't explain why a slender, white haired, pointy eared fictional elf featured in so much of my lustful fantasising when my usual type was of the big, beefy, dark haired rugby player ilk. Let's just not go there. This object of lust was an old friend of mine that I hadn't seen or heard of in a very long time, Rob. Let me tell you the story of how Rob and I got acquainted.

We had met about twenty years earlier when I was married to Phil, my childhood sweetheart. What a jolly cockup my one and only marriage had been but we learn from our mistakes right? We were living in Germany at the time, Phil was in the forces and we had a three year posting out there which on the whole was a riot. We had a great time, cheap beer, great summers, it was like one long holiday. Rob was the hubby's best friend and drinking partner.

I'll never forget the first time we were introduced. I was in the kitchen making something to eat and Phil walked in with this tall, dark haired, guy. "Hi hun" said Phil, slapping me on the arse "meet Rob, Rob this is Scarlett the Mrs."

I looked up from what I was doing straight into these amazing dark brown eyes and was lost. He looked straight back at me, holding out his hand, his mouth curled up in a sexy, lazy grin "Very pleased to meet you, Scarlett"

The sexual chemistry between us was immediate and intense, I'd never felt anything like it. He made me go weak at the knees, my mouth went dry and I was quivering, not unpleasantly, from the inside out. It's a good job I wasn't chopping veg at the time I think I would have lost a finger or two. I shook his hand, his touch making me tingle and barely managed to mumble a hello back. Luckily Phil had his head in the fridge looking for a beer or something to stuff in his face as usual otherwise I'm sure even he would have noticed my blushing face and the fact that I was trembling.

That night I dreamt about mad passionate sex with Rob and actually had an orgasm in my sleep, the first and only time this has ever happened to me. I must have been a little vocal because Phil commented with a grin over breakfast the next morning "Don't know what you were dreaming about last night but it sounded like you were having a right good time of it"

I managed to laugh, well less of a laugh and more of a guilty titter, as I lied and I told him I couldn't remember what I had been dreaming of. I was sure that he could see right into my dirty little mind where unbidden images of doing things I definitely should not with his best mate were running riot. I often talk in my sleep and for months lived in fear of shouting out Rob's name whilst dreaming about him which I often, and enjoyably did.

I was always amazed that no one else, especially Phil had ever noticed the effect that Rob and I had on each other. It always seemed so obvious and palpable, the atmosphere was sexually charged whenever we were in the same room together, the air thick with pheromones. Although we never discussed it, Rob and I both knew how we felt would inevitably lead to other things if we weren't careful and so tried to avoid being alone together at all costs. I told Phil I didn't like Rob all that much and made excuses to go out whenever he brought him round. We did do our very best to resist the temptation of each other, we knew it was wrong, but lust won in the end and we ended up having a crazy, dangerous and passionate affair which lasted for about six or seven months.

Ironically it was partially Phil's fault that the affair even came about. It was summertime, a few months after I first met Rob. Our time in Germany had come to an end and the regiment was headed back to England. With a months leave to look forward to we were going to stay with family for a few weeks before moving into our new quarters near Sailsbury. It turned out we were driving our car back on the same day that Rob had also planned to drive back. So we could all do the long trip in one haul Phil came up with the idea of sharing the driving of both cars between the three of us. He also suggested taking it in turns to be passengers in each other's cars so that we wouldn't fall asleep at the wheel. "I know you two don't particularly get on" he said to me "But it makes sense to do it this way and it's only for this trip".

He had absolutely no idea.

Consequently because of this arrangement there came a point on the lengthy journey where Rob and I were alone together in his car and it was game over. There was no conversation or discussion about how we felt, there was no need, he simply took hold of my hand without taking his eyes off the road and said "Saturday?"

"Yes" I replied, his touch electrifying me "I'll think of something."

He was staying at his parents for the next couple of weeks so he gave me their number. This was in the dark ages when only Wall Street traders owned mobile phones that were the size of shoe boxes so there were lots of clandestine trips to the telephone box that summer. Phil was staying with his mother for the first week we were home but as I didn't get along with the venomous old bitch I refused to stay there with him and was staying with my family which was the usual arrangement when we were on leave. Sneaking out to meet Rob for the first time didn't prove to be much of a challenge as Phil was six miles down the road no doubt being waited on hand and foot by mummy and being told for the thousandth time that I wasn't good enough for him. She'd have loved to have known about Rob and I. There would have been several smug "I told you so's"

Saturday crawled around at long last, the anticipation of seeing Rob almost killing me. I was an insane bundle of nerves and a complete bitch to everyone all week. I had constant conversations with myself in my head, telling myself it was wrong and I should leave well alone but I was completely powerless to resist. I couldn't eat, I couldn't sleep I burst into tears at least twice for no apparent reason. Mum asked me if I was pregnant about forty times and Dad kept muttering something under his breath about bloody women and hormones and threatening to call the men in white coats to come and take me away.

Rob had arranged to stay the night at a friend's flat, his friend was working night shifts so we had the place to ourselves. I told my parents I was going out with my friend Ellen and would be staying over at hers just in case Phil rang to speak to me and off I went. It took me a while to find it, dark ages remember - pre sat nav, but I finally arrived at the address Rob had given me. I sat outside in the car for a while, still a little undecided, knowing if I did this it could never be undone.

Finally I got out of the car and rang the doorbell trembling with nerves and desire.

He opened the door to me dressed in jeans and a white t-shirt, barefoot, dark hair wet from the shower and slicked back. He smelt great - clean and citrusy and very sexy. The sight and smell of him turned my legs to jelly. Grinning, he gestured for me to go inside. "Hello gorgeous, I didn't think you'd come" he said.

I grinned back, "I didn't think I would either" I admitted.

"I'm glad you did" he said bending down to kiss me.

We went inside. The place was a bit of a dump with peeling wallpaper, bare floorboards and junk shop furniture straight from the seventies. It was a hot night, even hotter in the claustrophobic, messy little flat. It smelt of damp, sweat, old food and cigarettes but none of that mattered, we were alone together at long last. In an effort at propriety we attempted to make conversation although it was obvious all we were interested in was sex. We were desperate just to rip each other's clothes off and get down to it. Rob ordered a takeaway which we pretended to eat whilst we gulped down the two bottles of cheap wine he had bought.

Of course it wasn't long before we got down to the real reason we were there and yes it was awesome. I had heard rumours that he was an amazing dancer, he certainly moved with an easy grace and confidence in the bedroom. He was also blessed with stamina and a large cock and he knew exactly what to do with it. That first time was just a frenzy, a release of the sexual tension that had been building up between us over the previous few months. There were no niceties, no kissing or foreplay, we didn't even make it to the bedroom. Conversation petered out, I couldn't have told you what we had been talking about if my life had depended on it. We just stopped talking, sat and looked at each other for a moment and then, as if pre-arranged, stood up at the same time, chairs tipping over in our hurry. There was no discussion he just quickly walked around behind me shoved my chair out of the way and whispered those three little words in my ear - "Bend over baby"

My annoying inner voice of reason told me I still had time to stop this but I ignored it. I was way, way past the point of no return. I did as Rob told me, pushing the plates of cold, congealing food out of the way and bending over the small table holding on to the sides. He pulled up my skirt and forced me further over the table until I was lay almost flat, my breasts uncomfortable on the hard top, my face turned to one side, cheek on the sticky surface. He pushed my knickers to one side and slid his cock inside me, then holding tightly to my waist with his big hands he began to fuck me. Slower, deliberate thrusts at first but soon turning hard and fast and dirty. I couldn't help but call out as I reached orgasm Rob climaxing quickly after me. It was pure animal lust and ecstasy. We stayed locked together for a few moments, then he withdrew gently lifting me from the table and turning me to face him. We kissed for a moment, him pushing my hair out of my eyes then he took my hand and led me into the bedroom where we just lay on the bed sweaty and out of breath.

We held hands and stared up at the ceiling not speaking for a while. There was a broken light fitting with cobwebs floating around it and I remember intently watching those cobwebs doing their lazy dance thinking to myself "I've just had sex with my husband's best friend" and wondering when the guilt would kick in.

We made love several times that night. The urgency of the first time gone, we went on to leisurely explore each other's bodies, kissing, caressing, licking, sucking, stroking and touching. Falling asleep for a couple of hours in each other's arms then waking up and doing it all over again. We were young and fit and just couldn't get enough of each other. We spent every moment together that we could over the next few days, I'd never had so much sex, he shagged me raw. The guilt never did kick in.

We were unable to meet up for a couple of weeks after that, as Phil spent the next week of leave with me at my parents then we were preoccupied with moving into our new place but it wasn't long before we managed to meet up again. Soon we were seeing each other almost every night. Getting more daring and taking stupid risks as time went on.

We continued to see each other for several months having sex at every available opportunity. As he was a single squaddie he lived on the barracks so most of the sex was hurried, half dressed squashed up on the back seat of his VW Golf which he would park up in one of the dark, secluded corners of the train station car park. There were no trains after 8pm in the little village where we lived so it was always deserted after then. I suddenly developed an interest in getting fit and bought a bike which of course was just a ruse to get out of the house for an hour or so each evening so I could meet Rob. I was doing plenty of riding alright but most of it was not on the bike. I also got a job at a local pub so I could see him after my shift ended, Phil never questioning why it took me two hours to get home sometimes after the bar closed.

It was a strange relationship, I certainly wasn't in love with him but I was definitely in lust. It was all about the sex. To be fair we didn't really do anything together apart from shagging so never got to know one another all that well. If we sneaked out to a neighbouring town for a drink we would have one, neck it as quickly as possible then go find somewhere to have sex. We didn't have much in common and I don't think we ever even had a full conversation but sexually we just couldn't get enough of each other. Although obviously he wasn't my first sexual experience, that particular trophy had gone to my husband, Rob was definitely the man who brought about my sexual awakening he made me realise just how great sex could be with the right partner.

How we kept it all a secret and never got caught I have no idea. We took some very dangerous risks. One night Phil had invited Rob over to our place for a drink and pizza. The close proximity of Rob was so irresistibly tempting that once I was sure Phil was asleep, I crept into the living room where Rob was on the couch, climbed on top of him and silently rode him, my heart pounding the whole time, only separated from my unsuspecting husband by a couple of feet and a thin plasterboard wall. We just couldn't help ourselves. The affair did eventually fizzle out when Rob met a single girl, a chubby glamorous blonde who couldn't have been physically more different to me and who of course I hated because I was insanely jealous of her stealing Rob. Then, when my rocky marriage irretrievably broke down not long after, I moved away and we lost touch.

I hadn't seen Rob in twenty years but had fantasised about him, his talented cock and some of the things we had gotten up to on plenty of occasions. Now, unbelievably after all this time there he was, large as life stood not ten feet away grinning right at me with a glint in his eye. Watching whilst I made a complete tit of myself singing about loving being spanked. I wrapped up my performance and blushing, walked over to him.

"Well, well, well" he said slowly applauding me, still grinning. "That was an amazing performance, so heartfelt. I believed every word you sang. It's a yes from me. Oh and I think I can help you out with someone mean and bossy!"

I laughed, utterly delighted to see him after all these years. "Rob White, what on earth are you doing here? It's so nice to see you!"

We embraced warmly, then stood back appraising one another. "Sexy as ever Scarlett" He said winking at me.

Him saying my name set a whole lot of fireworks off in my body. I blushed and muttered my thank you's. I've never been very good at taking compliments. He had lost some hair and put a bit of weight on but he still looked pretty good to me and of course still had those amazing, sexy dark brown eyes. The sexual chemistry was definitely still there, the air around us crackled with it.

CHAPTER 22

I couldn't help but wonder if fate had anything to do with Rob coming back into my life. Maybe we had been destined to be together all along but the timing just hadn't been right the first time around. Fortuitously it turned out that he was also single. He had married the chubby blonde that I had been so insanely jealous of and I couldn't help but feel a bit smug when he told me that the marriage hadn't lasted very long. Less than a year in fact. He had been married a second time and that marriage had lasted a good while longer than the first but he was now divorced again and had been single for the best part of two years.

There was still amazing chemistry between us so when he invited me out for dinner I didn't hesitate to accept. We met a couple of days later. It was a gorgeous summers evening and after a delicious meal where we caught up on what had been happening in each other's lives over the last twenty or so years we went for a leisurely walk along the canal. Although a bit more reserved than the younger me I still had the urge to just go somewhere private, rip our clothes off and shag for England but he seemed perfectly happy just to hold my hand, walk and talk.

A huge lump of disappointment stuck like a bone in my throat when he dropped me off at home later, not coming in, making his excuses saying sorry but he had an early start the next day. Maybe I was reading the signals wrong, maybe he didn't fancy me any more, maybe he just wanted to be friends? I did cheer up a little when we arranged another date for Thursday. Perhaps he was just playing things cool?

Thursday came around and I was very excited to see him. We had exchanged several messages and from the gist of those, some being rather racy, I came to the conclusion that yep, there was still chemistry between us I hadn't imagined it and he did still fancy me. But frustratingly the same thing happened that night. He was the perfect gentleman driving me home and walking me to my door after a very pleasant evening. Leaving me with nothing but a smile and a quick kiss before driving off. I was exceedingly pissed off. And horny. And frustrated. Why was he playing so hard to get? I yanked off my fancy lace underwear which had been stuck up my arse, annoying and itching me all night and totally pointless as no one had seen it but the cat, flung it on the floor, kicked it and told no one in particular to "Just fuck right off then!"

Walter, who was lay in his usual spot on my bed blinked at me, yawned, stretched then skulked off to go kill a mouse or something leaving me to enjoy my sexually frustrated induced bad mood in peace.

Rob messaged me the next day to ask what I was doing on Saturday. I did have plans to go out with the girls but thought surely he can't say he has to get off for an early start on the Sunday when he wasn't working? So I changed my plans and agreed to go out for a drink with him. He was going to come to my place and then we were going to get a taxi so he could have a drink. That meant he must be planning on staying as he wouldn't be able to drive home after a drink, happy days!

Saturday came and as arranged Rob turned up at mine around seven. He was looking particularly sexy in black jeans and white shirt which showed off his summer tan. He kissed me hello sending pleasant shocks of desire all around my body and giving me major ructions down below. I almost suggested forgoing the drink and just heading straight to bed but just about managed to keep my lust under control. Thankfully the taxi arrived before I lost it completely and was unable to stop myself from jumping on him and ripping his clothes off.

It was very busy, crowded and loud in the pubs. We watched a band in one then he took me to a place that had karaoke on and tried to convince me to sing Hanky Panky again for him which I laughingly declined to do. He was great fun to be with and insisted on buying the drinks all night. We had an awful lot to drink, it affecting me more because I'd been too nervous and excited to eat much that day. We grabbed a quick kebab at around 1am, something I would never even contemplate eating sober, jumped into a taxi and went home where we both quickly fell into bed and straight into a drunken coma with no sexual shenanigans whatsoever.

I woke up the next morning with the mother of all hangovers. Sex was the furthest thing from my mind because I had what felt like a brass band marching through my head and the slightest movement induced severe nausea. But it was very nice indeed to snuggle up to Rob and snooze most of the morning away together, just staggering to the bathroom occasionally to gulp down a gallon of water and a couple of paracetamol. I had missed Sunday morning naked cuddles and appreciated them even in the midst of death by alcohol poisoning.

We finally crawled out from under the covers at about 3pm and went out for a late lunch. A big tasty home cooked roast dinner down at the local helping take the edge off the hangover. He dropped me back off at home around 6 and said he would ring me. I was a little disappointed that there had been no sex again but had to accept that in reality neither of us had been in any fit state.

He rang as promised. We spoke to each other

and messaged every day and agreed to meet up on Wednesday for something to eat. Once again he made his excuses and we went our separate ways after the date. I was beginning to get very fed up at this point, here we were both single this time around, still fancied each other, the chemistry was definitely still there but nothing was doing in the bedroom department! What the hell was going on? I was beginning to imagine all kinds of things. He had lied to me and was actually still married, he had decided he was gay, he had taken a vow of celibacy, he simply didn't fancy me anymore?

I was enjoying his company and I was reasonably sure he was enjoying mine too. Maybe he just wanted a platonic relationship but our messages were flirty, full of innuendo, he seemed keen to spend time with me, our kisses were decidedly more than just friendly and I certainly didn't do naked cuddles with any of my other friends so why nothing doing on the sex front? Maybe he was playing it cool, not rushing things thinking he was being respectful? I just didn't know. The simple answer to my dilemma would be to just ask him what was going on but I'm a woman so I don't do simple! I'd much rather just let my imagination run riot and wind myself up with various incorrect scenarios than actually have a reasonable conversation and find out the truth.

We had arranged to meet again on Friday and I started to ask him if he wanted to stay at my house again so he could have a drink but then changed my mind and suggested maybe I could stay at his? He said he was fine with that so this at least answered my question as to his relationship status. If he was fine with me going over to stay with him then he obviously didn't have a significant other that he had forgotten to mention hidden away at home.

Friday came and I made an extra effort to look super sexy. I decided not to get drunk nor to let him get drunk either, I wanted my wicked way with him that night and I was very determined I was going to get it!

The night started well, we went for a curry and just had one bottle of wine between us. I made sure I took quite a long time over my meal and just sipped at the wine. After we had finished he suggested going on to a bar but I fluttered my eyelashes at him, gave him my best sultry smile and said "Why don't we just go home?" He looked a little reluctant but agreed.

Back at his place, he put some mellow music on, dimmed the lights and got us a glass of wine. "Well" I commented "you've certainly gone up in the world. This is a lot nicer that the first night we spent together." referring to the dingy, smelly flat where we had first had sex all those years ago.

He laughed "Yes" he agreed "it is a slight improvement."

"So, don't you want to bend me over the table again?" I asked. He just grinned at me. "That was a hint, just in case you didn't get it" I pointed out.

He laughed "Yeah" he said "I got it. I prefer the bed these days though, easier on the knees"

"Shall we go to bed then?" I asked

"No rush." he replied "Slow it down tiger. Let's finish our wine first."

Grr! I was half demented with desire. He was so close, he smelled so good, he looked great. Slow it down? This was the fifth time I had seen him and all we had done so far was kiss and cuddle. Never mind the niceties, I needed him to fuck me like he had done all those years ago, it's all I had been able to think about for the last two weeks.

I quickly drank my wine, sat twirling my empty glass in one hand, suggestively rubbing his thigh with my other and throwing meaningful looks his way.

"Do you want some more?" He asked nodding at my glass.

"No thanks"

What felt like fourteen frustrating hours later he finally, finally finished his drink. Taking my glass from me he put it on the coffee table with his, stood up and held out his hand. I took it, he pulled me up off the sofa then lead me into his bedroom. Standing by the bed we undressed each other slowly, kissing and touching as we did so. Down to our underwear he paused for a moment, he stood back and looked me up and down admiring my saucy knickers and stockings. Raising an eyebrow he grinned at me. "Nice" he said

"Now take them off."

I did as I was told without any argument.

Finally we both stood naked. I put my hand on his cock which was sporting a healthy erection, and gave it a gentle squeeze. "Hello there, I've missed you" I whispered bending down to kiss it.

He lay on the bed and pulled me down next to him. We kissed for a while and then he got on top of me. I felt his hardness gently pushing against me and then gasped at that sweet feeling as he entered me at long last.

Slowly he began to move inside me, it was heavenly for a moment but then he gave a sigh of frustration and I felt him going soft. He pulled out of me and rolled onto his back at the side of me. "I'm so sorry" he said his voice subdued with embarrassment "this happens occasionally."

I was beyond frustrated but what could I say? He was already embarrassed and it's not as if he had done it on purpose. I lay there worrying that it was my fault. "Is it me?" I asked "are you just not attracted to me anymore?"

"God no, it's not that" He replied reaching over and pulling me close to him "I still fancy you as much, if not more than ever. It's just something that happens from time to time. I'm just getting old, haha"

"It's OK, don't worry" I said magnanimously.

It wasn't OK though, I was fucking horny, I'd been horny for two weeks thanks to Rob and I desperately needed him to give me a good seeing to.

We cuddled for a while and started to kiss again. There was a little flicker of life so I massaged, stroked, licked, kissed and sucked for so long that it got embarrassing but it was all to no avail. I did my very best but that soldier was not standing to attention that night no matter what. Rob used his fingers and tongue and he did give me an orgasm which was OK and thankfully relieved some of my frustration but it was not the good sex I had been hoping for. The whole thing felt a little forced and like we had unfinished business.

"I am so sorry" He said "I'll get some Viagra for next time, hoping there will of course be a next time"

"Of course there will be a next time" I assured him, kissing him.

We kissed a while longer then fell asleep with him spooning me. I was sure everything would be OK, I was happy, apart from this little glitch it was all going so well. We would put our faith in the wonders of modern medicine and hope that that little blue pill would work it's magic.

As promised, the next time Rob came over to see me he had a packet of Viagra with him. It was one of those rare warm evenings you get sometimes in the late summer, so we opted to go out into the garden where we burnt some steaks on the little wobbly barbecue and had a couple of beers. Just the one each mind, didn't want anything possibly adversely affecting his performance later.

After we had eaten he took a pill and we took a long shower together washing each other all over and sharing some slow, lingering kisses. After towelling each other off we took it into the bedroom climbing naked and still a little damp into bed. It had been a good hour since he had taken the tablet but there was still no signs of life down below. Feeling disappointed but not wanting to put him under any extra pressure I just concentrated on the kissing and cuddling hoping that it was just delayed action. Sadly though after another hour or so we had to admit defeat. We tried everything we could think of, even resorting to watching some rather dodgy porn (do people actually get turned on by that crap?) but his dick stubbornly remained indifferent to all our efforts staying resolutely flaccid. It hadn't worked. I told him it didn't matter, we could try again another time and there were other things he could try. But really it did matter, we were both frustrated to hell and I think it was a long time before either of us fell asleep.

Over the following weeks his doctor prescribed other pills. There were about five different ones available and he tried them all but sadly they all had the same result - none of them worked. He was referred to a specialist who prescribed injections. These worked to a certain extent, they did give him an erection for a while but they were very painful to administer as he had to inject them directly into his penis. The sight of the needle was a passion killer. The idea of them totally destroyed his libido rendering the whole thing pointless. Frankly it put me off a bit too, I've never been very good with needles.

The problem quickly began to put a strain on our relationship. We were snappy with each other and began to argue over the stupidest of things. I think if we had been together longer than just a couple of months we probably would have worked at it a little harder but as it was the embarrassment and frustration on both sides caused by the situation just started to drive a wedge between us. We gave up trying to have sex in the end, eventually avoiding being in any kind of intimate situation, even the kissing stopped because it just ended up a humiliating exercise in failure every time.

The irony of the situation was almost too bitter to contemplate. It was almost as though we were being punished by the universe for our indiscretions all those years ago. The virile and insatiable young man I had happily shagged at every available opportunity behind my ex-husbands back now had droopy dick syndrome.

We had actually got to know each other quite a bit better this time around now it wasn't just all about a quick, illicit, shag. We got on really well, had a laugh and discovered we actually liked each other quite a lot. He was perfect for me in so many ways, ticked so many boxes, we enjoyed each other's company and I could have seen us having a happy, significant relationship if it wasn't for that one little problem. I know there are other ways to be intimate with someone but sex is important to me. I need a good sex life like I need food and air. Nothing beats making love with someone you care about and I knew that realistically I wouldn't be able to live without it in a relationship. But I didn't want to stop seeing him, I had genuine feelings for him that now went beyond lust and enjoyed his company but things couldn't possibly continue as they were. Our relationship was fast becoming one of just polite friends with an unhealthy dose of sexual frustration. The situation eventually resolved itself when Rob accepted a promotion at work which meant him moving almost two hundred miles away. There was no question of me going with him, I half suspected he only took the promotion as a way out of our relationship without either of us getting hurt by actually having to officially end it which was definitely on the cards.

When it was time for him to go we hugged for a long time making half hearted promises about keeping in touch and visiting each other but we both knew we were lying. I was so very sad and I missed him terribly. Why did life have to be so cruel? What had been the point of us reconnecting after all those years for it to end like that?

Fate kept teasing me first with Connor and then

with Rob. I felt as though I was destined to be alone forever, dating hopeless dickheads off POF or Tinder in my fruitless search for Mr Right with only the occasional shit shag to look forward to. The only orgasms coming courtesy of my friends with batteries.

CHAPTER 23

I tried to distract myself by going back on the dating sites after Rob moved away but my heart really wasn't in it. I hadn't used the apps for a while and had hidden my profiles so I unhid them and uploaded some new, more recent photos. Then I amused myself for a while looking through all the awful profiles on the various sites but couldn't find anyone I could be arsed messaging. The problem was, none of them could measure up to Rob or Connor.

I was still in touch with Chris and Pete but I hadn't spoken properly to either of them in several weeks not whilst I had been seeing Rob. Hadn't seen either of them not really given either of them much thought to be honest until I got a message off Chris -

Hey, not seen you for a while, fancy going out for something to eat some time soon, then coming back to mine and letting me eat your pussy for des sert :)? xx

Sweet message. Classic Chris. Oh sod it, why not, I thought. Chris was pretty good in bed and he would take my mind off Rob for a while I suppose.

But then another message arrived -

    Only problem is, you'll have to pay been sacked. lol :)

For fucks sake, again?! I'd had enough of this bollocks. I typed in the reply -

    Oh grow the fuck up you complete waste of time lazy pothead and wash your fucking disgusting sheets!!!!

but then deleted it and as I'm really a nice polite kind of person settled for the more diplomatic -

    No Chris, I won't be seeing you any more, sorry. Take care xx

And as for Pete, well it turned out that he'd been shagging one of my mates for months. Not that I actually gave two hoots about that but what I did mind was the fact that they fell out and dragged me into their argument.

Pete was a master of arrogant fuckery which of course I had known about all along and I had been having some suspicions about his relationship with Stacey. They pretended to hate each other whilst at the same time having an unnatural curiosity about one another. Each would ask me questions about the other in an overly casual way, "Are you still seeing that nob head Pete?" " Have you seen that weird friend of yours lately? What's she called?" pretending that they weren't really interested which is of course always a dead giveaway that they really are interested and have had or want to have intimate relations with each other.

He called her a fat, ugly, loony cunt (he really wasn't a nice person at all) and said he was pretty sure she was a lesbian. She called him a racist, misogynistic, nasty, selfish, arrogant twatwaffle which I have to agree was a pretty fair and accurate description.

They had actually met, coincidentally on POF prior to me and Pete meeting on there, although I didn't know until after the fact. They would only admit to meeting for the one date, saying they hadn't hit it off at all and both vehemently denied ever sleeping together. When Stacey found out I was seeing him she rolled her eyes and tried to warn me off him. "It's OK" I assured her "I'm only using him for sex. I know he's a bit of a bastard, but he's good in bed."

He would show me messages she had sent to him, asking him to go over, but claimed not to be interested in her. Then she would show me messages from him asking when he could come to see her but claimed not to be interested in him. I actually couldn't care less about the whole situation and whether or not they were shagging each other, frankly it was just tiresome. That was until they had a massive row over something he had posted on social media and I got unwillingly and unfairly dragged into it.

The row, as so often these things are, was over nothing but escalated into a ridiculous war between them. Stacey sent me a screenshot of a message from him lying to her saying I had been saying things to him about her that I most certainly had not. Then Pete sent me a screenshot of a message she had sent to him stating he must be desperate to be shagging me. Bloody charming. They were like a couple of sodding school kids. They'd most definitely fucked each other at some point. No one hated each other with as much venom as these two did unless sex was involved. I blocked the pair of them and left them to get on with it, I was far too old for this shit. No great loss on either count to be honest.

Anyway I was now as completely and utterly single as I could be and so I headed back to the dating sites. After a couple of non-starters like the bi-sexual guy who was into group sex and drinking breast mik, and an Egyptian ENT surgeon who was looking for someone to move in with him and his wife and have a baby that we could all share and love, I met Karl via Tinder.

He made it past the first date and we ended up seeing each other for a few weeks. He was very handsome, dressed smartly, nice shoes, was intelligent, funny and appeared to be loaded. I'm not quite sure how he funded his extravagant lifestyle and paid for his fancy cars and home as he didn't appear to work. I'd asked him once what he did for a living, not that it mattered particularly but I am just nosy. He just answered with a vague and dismissive "Oh, this and that." and the subject was closed.

Maybe he had won the lottery, had been left a fortune off a dead relative, or maybe he was a drug dealer. Or the secret love child of a member of royalty. Or a porn star, he certainly had the equipment and I have a vivid imagination.

He had a very impressive, tastefully decorated, big detached house out in the middle of nowhere and spoilt me with extravagant gifts, huge bouquets of flowers and meals out in fancy restaurants. We would have lovely chill out sessions which he called "double bubbles" in the hot tub in his massive garden under the stars with glasses of champagne, the real stuff not that cheap wannabe fizzy wine crap. His hot tub was a proper job built into a deck not one of those blow up efforts. Although I don't consider myself to be particularly materialistic it was a lifestyle I happily embraced and could quite easily have become accustomed to.

He was very skilled between the sheets, knew how to please a lady and was pleasingly more than adequately endowed. He was also camper than a row of tents and I did wonder from time to time about his sexuality. I know lots of heterosexual men who are quite camp and in touch with their feminine side but he took it to a whole new level entirely.

Handsome, rich, well endowed, intelligent, generous - OK so what was the deal here? Why was this very eligible man still single? So he was more than a bit camp? Was that really such a deal breaker when he so much more on offer?

Well personally I could probably have coped with the campness, it was certainly outweighed by all the positives on offer, but the catch was the dog. I was no match for that little bitch. Karl was one of life's weird and wonderful eccentrics, more than a little bit strange maybe, but a pleasant enough guy. He was good company and perhaps, if it hadn't been for the demon dog, things might have worked out between us. I was certainly enjoying being spoilt, it made a nice change from the indifferent selfishness of fuck and go Pete and the perpetual poverty that Chris existed in because he was forever getting sacked and spending all his money on weed.

But that fucking dog. She, a horrible, yappy, evil little Yorkshire terrier called Betty was the unquestionable love of his life.

Betty was beyond spoilt, she had her hair done more often than I did. She was forever at the groomers having blueberry face masks (yes, these really are a thing) and spa baths and fluffy blow dries and was always dressed in cute little sparkly outfits. She was like a canine version of those disturbing American beauty pageant kids. She had more clothes and hair accessories than Primark. Karl hand fed her minute slices of home cooked chicken and steak, called her "Betty Baby Cakes" and told her he loved her often and in a disturbing falsetto voice. He would pick her up, alarmingly squeal "Daddy loves you!" and shower her with noisy lip smacking kisses rather frequently. Don't get me wrong, I love animals but this over the top show of affection was more than a bit off-putting to be honest.

Of course Betty the spoilt demon bitch dog from hell took an instant and intense dislike to me and tried to bite me on several occasions. Sometimes even succeeding with a nasty little nip if I wasn't quick enough. Karl would just laugh and say indulgently "Oh stop it you naughty, jealous little girl. Daddy still loves you." To me he would say "Don't worry she's only playing, the little minx!" but I wasn't so sure. I could tell she was plotting my demise in that tiny but sharp, evil, conniving little canine brain of hers. I wondered how many of Karl's previous girlfriends had been savaged by the small, admittedly cute but evil beast.

Even though Betty had her own princess themed bedroom with miniature four poster bed (I'm not joking) she had pride of place on Karl's king sized. She was a constant presence. Even when we were making love he didn't kick her out of his room. She would be right there watching the proceedings, glaring at me with utter contempt. She had no morals that dog, no shame whatsoever.

I stayed over a few times and I would wake up in the night to find her disturbingly staring right at me, her beady little black eyes boring into me. She'd be quietly growling and showing her small but very sharp nasty teeth in an evil little grin. I would quietly growl back and whisper at her to fuck right off but she scared me, I swear she had supernatural powers. I was convinced she had somehow possessed Karl. I began to fear for my face when I was sleeping.

Although, apart from being a reluctant and uncomfortable exhibitionist for the voyeuristic Betty, the sex was great and despite the fact that I was more than happy to be spoilt and really enjoyed Karl's company I decided in the end the strange business with the dog was all just a little bit too much. The thing that finally finished it off for me was the time we went out for a walk and he produced a bright pink doggy pram that he took her out in. I had no idea such things existed. He considered that she was far too precious to actually walk on the outside ground. Or go on a lead. It was her birthday that day too apparently and he'd had a new collar made especially for her. Pink of course with little crystals (or maybe even real diamonds, he was mad enough) spelling out her name and a huge three tier dog edible birthday cake.

I had to accept that actually he was beyond merely eccentric and was actually totally insane. Nice enough guy but a complete fruit loop. Far too much of a nutter, even for me. Shame really.

So back to the joy of the internet dating sites I went. My following three dates went a bit like this...

Matt

Him "Are you into water sports?"

Me "I tried to water ski once but it was an absolute disaster, I ended up involuntary drinking half the lake! I do swim a lot though."

Him "No, I mean *water sports*..."

Me "Huh?"

Him, slowly "Do you like...To be... Pissed on?"

Me "Erm, no, not really. Can't say it's ever really appealed."

Him "Would you like to piss on me?"

NEXT...

Darren.

I met Darren in a bar and all was going well, until he whispered in my ear that sexy women's underwear turned him on. Great, I like to wear nice knickers so I had no issues with that. Then he told me he was wearing hold ups and a thong. I laughed "Hahaha! Very funny"

He was six foot four, buzz cut, tattooed, twenty or so stone of muscular firefighter. I thought he was having a joke. I was waiting for him to laugh with me. Nope. He was deadly serious. He was glaring at me, his face like granite.

Now, I'm definitely no prude and although I admit the whole modern gender / sexual identity thing sometimes confuses me a little, I am all for equality and acceptance across all the multiple types that people identify with nowadays. People could be what they wanted. Shag who they wanted (as long as it was legal and consensual of course) look like and dress in whatever the hell they bloody well wanted to as far as I was concerned. But I knew that if this very masculine guy stripped off to a lacy thong and hold-ups in my presence I probably wouldn't be able to stop my face from smiling loudly because that's just how I'm made. Inappropriate mirth is one of my many skills. And that would most likely upset or piss him off a bit.

NEXT...

Clive.
Him "Are you still on the dating sites?"
Me "Um, yes."
Him "So you're on a date with me, but you're still on the dating sites?"
Me "Errr, yeah. It is only our first date."
Him "Are you some kind of cunt?"
Me "Excuse me?"
Him "You are obviously a fucking slag. I want nothing more to do with you."
Walks out the bar.
For fucks sake. BLOCK!

CHAPTER 24

Weekend again, another lonely single Saturday night. I had no money to go out, was bored stupid and there was nothing entertaining to watch on the telly. I'd not been on any new dates for a while, frankly I was beginning to find the whole thing exhausting and I hadn't bothered to check the dating sites for any new messages in several days. I decided to log into them to see if there were any potential new victims.

I had several messages from the usual selection of fuckwits, sexual predators and not rights on POF, a match on Tinder that I didn't remember swiping right on, I must have been drunk at the time and wearing beer goggles, or maybe I'd missed him when I deleted all my accidental right swipes because he really wasn't my type at all. Three chins, hairy nostrils, missing teeth, the most awful neck tattoo I'd ever seen. He'd sent me an uninspiring message "Hey Sexy" with a winking emoji - yawn. I unmatched him. Rude maybe but I was beyond caring any more.

I also had a couple of new messages on OKCupid. One was a definite no, just not my type at all. The other guy looked alright though. Not really my usual type looks wise but his profile was interesting and I liked what he had wrote.

We matched quite highly on the percentage score thingy that OKCupid did based on questions you answered. We were 97% compatible apparently. I did consider this compatibility thing to be a bit of bullshit really especially after getting to know some of guys I was supposedly highly compatible with and finding out we had zero in common, but I noticed with interest that we had given a lot of the same answers in the sex category. Hmmm..

His message was nice, a little generic but polite with a bit of humour so I decided I would message him back. Why not? He would probably turn out to be yet another to add the long and ever increasing list of disappointing dates but I was doing nothing else and I was bored.

He was called Ben and we exchanged the usual pleasantries via messaging for a few minutes. He explained to me that his personal situation was quite unusual and asked if we could possibly chat on the phone so there could be no ambiguity or confusion. I admit to being a little intrigued. OK in truth I'm just bloody nosey, and as I said I was bored so although I didn't usually give out my number this early in the game I agreed to a call.

We chatted for literally hours on the phone. Ben's situation was indeed highly unusual, he couldn't offer any commitment but that was fine. It actually appealed to me as I wasn't really looking for anything serious. I was looking to get laid not married.

He sounded genuine and his story believable. He was very polite, well spoken, seemed intelligent and I found myself warming to him. I am not sure how we got onto the subject but he started to tell me a little about his sexual history and experiences. Oh boy did the conversation then start to get interesting. He had got to be, hands down the most sexually experienced man I had ever spoken to in my whole life.

He explained, though not recently, he had been a very prolific and enthusiastic participant on the swinging scene for several years. Most of his long term relationships had been suited to this lifestyle with his partners willingly joining in the fun.

He alternatively shocked and entertained me with several stories from his past. I admitted to him that I'd always been very curious about swinging and he asked me if I'd like to go to a club with him just to see what it was like not necessarily to get involved in any erm, activities. He promised that if I went with him he would look after me, make sure no harm came to me and that I wouldn't have to put up with any undesirable attention. He also promised me it would be nothing like I had imagined. At that point my dirty little mind was getting carried away with itself picturing something like the Frankie Goes to Hollywood "Relax" video setting, a hedonistic orgy palace with whips and chains and cages and people performing sexual acts and shagging each other every which way at every turn.

I was very intrigued by this man and this lifestyle he was describing, but also a little wary and undecided about meeting up. I was excited about the possibility of exploring new experiences and discovering new facets of my sexuality, but I was wondering was this really for me? Was he for me? Could this be the amazing but so far elusive sex that I had been searching for? I knew I was a little kinky and had always had a healthy sexual appetite but was this above my level of kink? Well, there was only one way I was going to find out I suppose but something, I guess my ingrained sense of propriety, conditioned by my upbringing and what I had been told was considered normal and acceptable by general society was holding me back a little.

During the course of our telephone conversation he had claimed to be very well endowed and the next morning I received a message from him politely asking if he could send me proof of his claim "Would you be offended if I sent you a picture of my penis to prove what I was saying about my size is true?"

I briefly pondered this strange message. With the exception of Pete who had liked to send me a picture of his pride and joy at least once a week, I hadn't yet been sent any dick pics. This was despite being assured I would be inundated with them when I joined the dating sites and I was feeling a little left out, haha! Joking apart though, would this mean I was shallow if the deciding factor to meeting Ben was based on the size of his tackle? He wasn't the best looking guy, maybe this was how he got women to go on dates with him. Ah sod it, I was curious, why not? Let's have a gander.

To be truthful I wasn't expecting much, a lot of men are very proud of their dicks and seem to be under the impression that they are bigger than they actually are. It's like the height thing. 5ft 6 seems to increase to 5ft 11 on their profile description. Perhaps they think we won't notice the missing inches that only exist in their imagination but we do boys, oh we do!

Anyway I sent a message back saying "send away!" and received in return not a picture but a short video showing it off in all of its turgid glory.

Well, what can I say? He was certainly under no illusions or fantasies here, he was truly, truly blessed in the trouser department. I've never seen anything quite like it outside of a porn film. We are talking length AND girth here ladies, eye watering. I couldn't help wondering what riding that big boy would feel like. I eagerly messaged back and arranged to meet him - of course I did, shallow, greedy bitch that I am!

We were both eager to meet up so made arrangements to meet the next evening at a nice hotel about half way between where we both lived. He was already there when I arrived, sat in the bar area and I spotted him before he saw me. If I am to be completely honest I did have a bit of a wobble and briefly considered leaving before he saw me. There was nothing wrong with him as such. OK so he was not tall dark and handsome but he was not vomit inducingly ugly either. He was clean, casually but nicely dressed, had nice shoes on, it was just that physically he wasn't what I would consider to be my usual type. I had met guys with similar builds to Ben and I just never felt any chemistry there. It was usually the big, tall, beefy guys that did it for me, probably because I'm not exactly dainty myself. I knew what his build was like from his profile pictures, so what had I been thinking? Oh yeah, as his video and wealth of sexual experience sprang to mind, that's what I was thinking. Maybe he was big and beefy just right where he needed to be.

Anyway, it was too late to sneakily disappear by then as he had glanced up and noticed me. I thought I can be polite and at least have a drink with him then make my excuses to leave if it wasn't going well or if there was no chemistry. I took a deep breath, plastered a smile to my face and walked over to him. He stood up as I approached and smiled back at me. He had a lovely, genuine inviting smile, nice eyes and very unthreatening aura about him. This was the sex mad swinger? I wasn't quite sure what I had been expecting but he looked so ordinary and nor-mal! I felt his eyes flicker quickly over my body in a subtle appraisal. I think he was pleased with what he saw and I noticed his smile broadened as he looked back at my face, his tongue briefly flicking over his bottom lip. My own smile broadened in response and I found it extremely difficult not to let my eyes wander down to his crotch! We greeted each other with polite "hello, pleased to meet you"s and he went to the bar to get me a drink.

We had a drink, a meal, more drinks and chat-ted non-stop for hours. Although we did cover the polite, generic what do you do for a living kind of questions our conversation, not surpris-ingly, was mostly about sex. There wasn't much he either hadn't tried or didn't know about. We discussed swinging, BDSM, sub-dom relation-ships, threesomes, foursomes and moresomes. Sex toys, the strangest places we had done it and with whom. Anal sex, oral sex, different positions... goodness knows what anyone would have thought had they overheard our conversa-tion.

We didn't kiss, we hardly touched and yet it was hands down the horniest date I have ever been on in my whole life. It was extremely difficult to stick to my no sex first date rule. He had an amazing personality and I could totally under-stand how and why he was so successful with the ladies. He looked at me like I was the most beautiful thing he had ever set eyes on, listened to me intently like I was the most interesting person he had ever met. He certainly was one of the most interesting people I'd ever met. He was polite almost to a fault, complementary but not in a creepy way. Charismatic, intelligent, very confident, especially in his sexuality, but not in the least bit arrogant.

The chemistry between us took me by surprise. It was amazing and intense. Pheromones were flying all over the place. I was very confused. My nether regions were twitching and I was actually squirming in my seat. He briefly brushed against my arm and I felt like I'd been electrocuted. He politely asked if he could touch my skin to see if it was as soft as it looked. I let him stroke my back a little under my top and I almost came right there just from that touch. All I could think about was getting a room and getting down and dirty for the next several hours with this guy, I just knew I wouldn't be disappointed. By the look on his face I think Ben was thinking the same thing.

It got late, then later, then very late. We eventually agreed we had to go and finally left the hotel. He walked me to my car and we shared a quick, chaste kiss in the car park. No more than a peck really, me becoming inexplicably shy and then we said our reluctant goodbyes and went our separate ways. I drove home far too fast, hornier than I've ever been in my whole life. I definitely would have been guilty of driving without due care and attention, I couldn't concentrate. I don't know how I didn't have an accident. When I got home it was the toy box or a cold shower. I chose to delve into the toy box. I could hardly wait to see him again.

CHAPTER 25

It was two days later when I met up with Ben again. He had convinced me to go to a local swingers club with him. I didn't know how to feel about it. I was nervous, very horny, slightly mortified and intrigued all at the same time. I think I was four parts terror, two parts excitement and one of bemusement.

He picked me up at the hotel and when I saw him I marvelled again at the chemistry I felt between us. How was this very ordinary looking and unassuming man having this profound affect on me?

"Are you OK?" He asked "Sure you want to do this? I don't want you to feel pressured into doing something you are not comfortable with."

I assured him I was fine with it, I definitely wanted to go. He smiled at me squeezed my thigh setting off the fanny flutters and then drove us the few miles to the club.

The club was nothing at all like I was expecting. The entrance very discreet, no signage. I never would have even known it was there. It was nowhere near as seedy inside as I thought it was going to be. It was very clean and tastefully decorated. There was a wet area with a small plunge pool, a large jacuzzi, sauna and showers, just like being in the wet area of a gym if you disregarded the naked people wandering around - oh and the fact that most gyms don't have a dungeon room. The dungeon room was well equipped for the use of those who enjoyed a bit of BDSM, think cages, handcuffs, belts, swings, chains, etc. For the voyeuristic the dungeon ceiling was made of thick glass so you could watch the proceedings from above if that was your thing.

The rest of the upstairs was set out just like an ordinary pub or club with a bar, pool table and brown leather chesterfield couches. There were a couple of differences such as (very badly acted) porn playing on the TV's, a mirrored stage with a pole and fish bowls full of condoms on the bar. There were a few people milling around some naked, some of the men with towels wrapped around them, some of the women in sexy underwear but there was nobody getting up to anything x-rated in the public areas, well not that night anyway. Sex was frowned upon in the general areas I was told although it was not unheard of.

For sex, on this floor there were private rooms, rooms with peep holes or two way mirrors, a couples only room and an anything goes orgy area. Think huge round bed, Romanesque pillars and side benches for spectators. Ben gave me the guided tour, holding my hand and explaining the unwritten rules as we went along. When he showed me the couples room there was a couple in there going at it. It was the first time I had ever seen anyone openly having full on sex right in front of me in real life but strangely it didn't feel weird to see them. I can't say watching them really did much for me as a turn on, I think at that point I was still a little too nervous, but it was interesting to discover I didn't find it either repulsive or embarrassing.

So there I was, stripped to my fancy underwear, in an environment that was very, very new and strange to me with a man who was almost a complete stranger, talk about being completely out of your comfort zone. At first I was feeling very self-conscious but to my surprise I soon found myself beginning to relax and start to enjoy myself. The people in the club were just your everyday, normal, ordinary folk. All ages and shapes and sizes. We chatted to a few people but made it clear we weren't interested in playing and no one forced the issue. The ambiance of the place was very chilled and uninhibited, everyone was very friendly but not overly so. Although there were subtle appraisals of my body from both male and female, which I admit was mutual, nobody stared at me nor made me feel uncomfortable or self-conscious. I was actually feeling quite liberated and very horny.

The main reason I was starting to enjoy myself,

and the reason I was feeling horny was because I was with Ben. I felt safe with him and knew he would fend off any unwanted advances. He was very attentive towards me and we had some very pleasurable, erotic moments in the wet area. In addition to his sizeable assets I discovered he had very talented hands and was an amazing kisser. We kissed and caressed each other like a couple of horny teenagers, had a very steamy, intimate necking session in the pool, no chaste, shy little kisses that night. I was beginning to feel a little crazy with desire and luckily it wasn't long before Ben suggested we go somewhere a little more private. I eagerly agreed and taking my hand he led me up to a private room.

This was certainly a very different first sexual encounter for me and one I'm hardly ever likely to forget. I was soon completely naked, lay on my towel, on a red PVC covered bed in a hot tiny room with mirrors on all four walls and the ceiling, it was hardly a place to be shy, body conscious or particularly romantic. This was all about the sex, nothing more, nothing less.

Ben took his time, starting off by leisurely stroking, kissing and licking my body all over. And I mean ALL over. No nook or cranny was left unexplored. I was squirming with pleasure and a little embarrassment, I wasn't used to my body being under such close scrutiny but every nerve ending was tingling with desire, longing and anticipation.

Whispering in my ear telling me what he was going to do to me he ordered me to get on all fours. I did as I was told feeling very exposed. He then started to pay particular attention to my arse. I was a little repulsed by this at first and worried to death I would accidentally fart but I forced myself to relax and try to enjoy it, after all the night was all about new experiences. I have always been a little OCD about personal cleanliness and so was very glad we'd been in the jacuzzi and pool beforehand and all my bits were chlorine clean otherwise I think I'd have been a little worried, especially when he didn't stop at licking and forced his tongue right up there. I almost yelped with shock and surprise, but it was actually very pleasant indeed and a massive turn on. For those of you who have never tried this before you go "ewww!" as I undoubtedly would have prior to this experience, let me assure you, you don't know what you are missing out on. Not for everyone maybe but it felt amazing, rude, dirty, horny as hell.

By this point I was massively turned on, literally shaking with desire and desperate for him to fuck me, especially after seeing his impressive cock which was rock hard. Thankfully it wasn't long before he obliged. He told me to lie down and gently turned me so I was half on my side, kissing my neck and nibbling on my earlobe sending a frisson of pleasure down my spine and all the way to my toes. "I'm going to fuck you now" he whispered into my ear and I quivered with anticipation, extremely pleasant twinges in all the right places.

He rubbed the smooth head of his cock against me teasing a little. I was a bit worried at first that he may hurt me but I was very wet and totally ready for him. It was nothing other than delicious when he stopped rubbing and instead pushed against me slowly slipping inside making me gasp. He asked me if I could take any more, yes I told him greedily. I wanted all of it. Carefully, slowly he pushed in deeper, filling me up, stretching me, a small amount of pain only adding to the overall pleasure.

I groaned involuntary as my orgasm began to build and he asked me if I was OK. I assured him I was more than OK and begged him not to stop. Grabbing my hair and pulling it gently, kissing and gently biting my neck he increased the speed of his thrusts pushing me to the most intense orgasm I had ever experienced. It erupted throughout my entire body, wave upon wave of pure pleasure, each thrust intensifying it further until I couldn't help but scream out. He brought me to orgasm two more times before he climaxed and afterwards we lay in a sex induced euphoria, spent, panting and sweating in that small, hot room.

"Now you know what it's like to be fucked properly by a real man" he whispered as he lay spooning me and stroking my skin.

Had I finally, after my long search, met my sexual soulmate? From first impressions it seemed that way. Let's just say I was very eager to find out. I became addicted to sex with Ben and we started to see each other on a regular basis. That night in the swingers club was just the beginning of a strange but interesting journey of sexual exploration together which would take me out of my comfort zone many more times and which eventually developed into something very intimate, intense and ultimately heartbreaking. But that, my friends, is another story entirely.

Not The End

CONFESSIONS OF A SERIAL DATER

Follow Scarlett on her journey looking for love and more importantly great sex, something that has been missing from her life for far too long.

Delete, Block, Next...

Meet Scarlett. Newly single, disillusioned with love, skint, wrong side of 40, a bit fat but amazing tits.

Negotiating the pitfalls of modern dating looking for a satisfying tumble between the sheets a couple of times a week with someone who's face doesn't want to make her vomit.

There appears to be plenty on offer but after weeding out the not rights, the scammers, the clinically insane and those with significant others just looking for a bit on the side the pickings are actually a little meagre.

Will she find what she is looking for or is she condemned to life of s***t sex the only orgasms coming courtesy of her friends with batteries?

Ever dated? Ever had sex? Ever been stupidly drunk? Then this is the story for you.

A funny, modern day satire about ordinary people and the weird and wonderful world of on-line dating, affairs, relationships, lust and embarrassing drunken behaviour. Kind of Fifty Shades meets Bridget!

Playing By The Rules

After a year of dating mishaps and romantic disasters Scarlett finally meets Ben. He's not much to look at but he's certainly providing her with the exceptional sex life she's been craving. Hurrah!

The only problem is he keeps trying to push her further out of her comfort zone, she's convinced he's lying to her about his personal life and she thinks she may be falling in love with him.

How far will she go to keep hold of him? Will she find out the truth he's been hiding from her? And who the hell keeps sending her the weird gifts that are getting stranger and stranger...

(Publishing date 29/04/2020)

Printed in Great Britain
by Amazon